Ohio Reading Circle
1979 6th

Trapped on the Golden Flyer

Trapped
on the Golden Flyer

BY

SUSAN FLEMING

Illustrated by Alex Stein

THE WESTMINSTER PRESS

PHILADELPHIA

Book Design by Dorothy Alden Smith

First edition

Published by The Westminster Press ®
Philadelphia, Pennsylvania

PRINTED IN THE UNITED STATES OF AMERICA

9 8 7 6 5 4 3 2 1

Library of Congress Cataloging in Publication Data

Fleming, Susan, 1932–
    Trapped on the Golden Flyer.

    SUMMARY: The train carrying Paul west through the Sierra Nevadas becomes frozen to the tracks during a blizzard and the passengers are drawn together in a fight for survival.
    [1. Survival—Fiction. 2. Railroads—Trains—Fiction. 3. Blizzards—Fiction] I. Stein, Alex. II. Title.
PZ7.F623Tr   [Fic]   77-15941
ISBN 0–664–32627–7

To my three train lovers,
Donald, Eric, and Gregory

CONTENTS

In January, 1952, a Southern Pacific passenger train, The City of San Francisco, was marooned for three days in the Sierra Nevada Mountains. TRAPPED ON THE GOLDEN FLYER is based on that incident. However, the story was not written as history. All the characters are fictitious, and the events described have been embellished by the author's imagination.

1
The Journey Begins

PAUL wanted to scream or cry. But a boy his age isn't supposed to scream or cry. So he stood quietly in the middle of the crowded station waiting room, his father's arm resting lightly around his shoulders.

Under his winter coat and heavy wool sweater, Paul shrank away from the protection of that arm. It made him mad because he couldn't depend on it anymore. He wanted to shrug it off, but he was afraid of hurting his father's feelings.

In less than an hour, he would be on his own. Alone on a train with strange people, going to a strange place where he would be met by strangers. If only he could go home. Go home and play checkers at the kitchen table with his dad. Or sing, "Casey would waltz with the strawberry blonde," while they did the dishes together.

Paul picked up his suitcase. His father would carry it to the train for him. But when he got to Oakland, would he be able to carry it by himself? He lifted it off the floor a few inches and held it a minute before

11

putting it down again. It was heavy. He could carry it, but he hoped he wouldn't have to carry it far.

The tan suitcase with wide brown stripes on each side had frayed leather bindings. Its leather handle was almost black from the many hands that had held it. Paul remembered his mother dragging the suitcase from under her bed every Thanksgiving, because she kept her linen tablecloths and napkins in it. She would wipe off the dust from the top of the case, snap it open, and carefully select the right cloths. He had always sat on the double bed watching her. His job had been counting out the napkins.

Paul didn't have any brothers or sisters, and his father didn't have any either. His mother's only sister was in California. All the grandparents had died, so the Sullivans never had any family to help them celebrate Thanksgiving, but they invited as many friends as their apartment would hold. Except for last year, of course, when Thanksgiving dinner was hot dogs and cole slaw at the counter of Benjie's Diner. With his mother so sick in the hospital, nobody felt like celebrating. Christmas had been even worse.

A voice came over the station loudspeaker. "Golden Flyer now ready for boarding. Golden Flyer. . . . Seven o'clock train for Omaha, Cheyenne, Green River, Ogden, Reno, Sacramento, Oakland, and San Francisco. Now boarding."

The words hit Paul in the stomach. He looked up at his father. "Is that my train?"

"That's it. Let's go."

They joined the great flood of people, who had been sitting on benches, standing around, or resting

12

on their suitcases, as they surged forward toward the Golden Flyer.

Paul felt like a leaf in a moving stream. He wanted to stop. He wanted to go back. But he couldn't resist the current that swept him forward, swirling around loaded baggage carts, rushing, pushing, on and on down the long platform toward the streamliner that would carry him to Oakland.

Daddy! Daddy! Take me home with you. Don't send me away. The words pounded inside his head, kept time to the rhythm of his feet running on the concrete platform to keep up with his father's long strides. But he did not speak the words. They wouldn't be heard. Couldn't be. Not above the hubbub of voices, the hissing from the cars, and the powerful throbbing of engines.

A cloud billowed up from under one of the cars and closed over Paul. He grabbed for his father's sleeve. Was the train on fire?

No, this was steam, not smoke, Paul told himself. The escaping steam that made the hissing sound came from the pipes that heated the train. In a moment he was beyond the cloud, and his father was steering him toward a coach car.

"Watch your step there." A blue-uniformed trainman put his hand under Paul's elbow to help him up the first high step of the car. The door into the coach was closed. But his father leaned against the bar across the middle, and it opened with a loud swoosh. Mr. Sullivan pushed the door back far enough so that it locked into an open position. He led the way down the aisle. It was jammed with people shoving their suitcases onto the overhead rack, taking off coats, giving last-minute instructions to a friend or relative.

"Don't forget to write."

"Give my love to Gertrude."

Mr. Sullivan stopped about halfway down the car. "Here's your seat, Paul. It's right next to the window. Do you want me to put your suitcase on the rack? Or would you rather have it on the floor where you can get at it easier?"

I'd rather have it at home under the bed where it belongs, Paul thought. Aloud he said, "I don't care."

"You won't have room for your feet if I leave it on the floor. I'll put it on the rack for you. Okay?"

"Okay."

"Don't worry. Everything'll be all right. Your Aunt Edith and Uncle Harold will be in Oakland to meet you Sunday. Have you got those sandwiches I made for you?"

Paul nodded.

"Better check."

"I don't have to check. I remember putting them right on top in my suitcase."

"You're sure?"

"I'm sure."

Mr. Sullivan reached into his overcoat pocket and pulled out the bag of peanuts and the magazine that he had bought in the station. "I almost forgot to give you these. They'll help you while away the time."

Paul put the peanuts and magazine beside him on the seat. "What are you going to do when you leave?"

"Just go home and go to bed. I've got to be at the station early tomorrow. I think I'll have traffic duty."

14

"You going to stop downstairs and talk to Mrs. Flaherty a while?"

"I guess I'll tell her you got off okay. Look, I gotta go. The train will be pulling out soon."

Paul tried desperately to think of something to keep his father with him a few minutes longer. But his mind was a blank.

"I gotta go. Be a good boy, now. You're going to like California. No snow and cold out there." Awkwardly and hurriedly, his father bent down and kissed the top of his forehead. "Good-by, Son," he said softly. He turned away quickly and headed out of the car.

"Good-by, Dad," Paul called to the familiar gray-coated back.

His father turned at the door. "I'll wait on the platform until the train leaves."

Paul looked out of the window and saw his own reflection and the brightly lighted platform at the same time, like a double exposure photograph. If he leaned close to the glass and cupped his hands around his eyes, he could see only the platform. His father appeared under the window, smiling up at him.

"Daddy! Dad!" Paul called. His father waved and moved his lips, but Paul couldn't hear what he was saying.

Paul raised his voice. "Dad, can you hear me?"

Obviously not, because Mr. Sullivan's expression didn't change and his lips didn't move in reply.

Paul wondered if he should run to the vestibule between the cars and talk to his father from there.

15

What would he say? Daddy, I love you. Don't leave me. Don't send me away.

But you can't yell that stuff so the whole train can hear. He decided to stay put.

Paul continued to look out at his father, who looked back at him every little while and smiled. But after a time he felt silly just staring out that way, and he leaned against the back of the blue upholstered seat and noisily blew out a long breath.

Waiting for the train to go was something like sitting in his mother's hospital room, waiting for her to die. After Thanksgiving she had barely recognized him. She was in so much pain that the doctors kept her drugged all the time. He would be in the room with her and yet he wasn't really with her at all. She couldn't talk to him anymore and she didn't even look like herself. He would stare at the plant, which Mrs. Flaherty had sent, with the petals that looked like purple and white velvet and try not to think or feel anything.

This was almost worse. He was separated by steel and glass from his father who was warm and alive and yet unable to talk to him. Move, train, get going, Paul thought. If I've got to go away, let me get it over with.

"But why do I have to go to live with Aunt Edith and Uncle Harold?" he had asked one night when they were having supper.

"There's no one to take care of you, Paul."

"You're here, Dad."

"But what about the times I have to work the night shift? I leave soon after you come home from school

16

and I'm not home again until after midnight. Where are you going to go when I'm not here?"

"I'll be okay. I won't get into any trouble."

His father had laid down his fork and looked straight at him with steady brown eyes. "Paul, look. You're a good boy and I want you to stay good. Chicago's no place for a kid to be running loose. I'm a cop. I know what goes on."

"I can stay downstairs with Mrs. Flaherty when you're not here."

"God save us, no! Mrs. Flaherty has five kids of her own and she doesn't know where *they* are half the time. She can't be looking out for you too."

At last the train began to move slowly ahead. Paul cupped his hands around his eyes for a last look at his father. He saw that the train had already moved almost a car's length away from the spot where his father was standing. "Good-by, Dad," he yelled through the window.

His father waved and looked as if he were saying something. Paul waved frantically back. He heard the trainmen banging down the metal platforms over the steps and shutting the outside doors. The Golden Flyer glided smoothly out of the station and into the bleak January night. Paul's journey had begun.

2

Mrs. Green Dress

WITHIN SECONDS all sight of his father was gone. Then the station was left behind, and the darkness outside mirrored Paul's face in the coach window.

He looked at his watch. It wasn't an expensive watch, but it was special because it had been his father's Christmas present to him. He still wasn't used to the feel of it on his wrist. It read 7:05. In 37 hours and 26 minutes he would arrive in Oakland to begin his new life. A new year—1955. A new life.

The train gathered speed, pulling him away faster and faster from all that was familiar. He shut his eyes and in his mind went back home with his father, back to the little room off the living room that was his, a room only big enough for his bed, a straight-backed chair, and a tall bureau which his mother had painted green. The wheels of the powerful streamliner rolled along the cold steel rails, licking up the miles, licking up the miles.

Paul tried to hang on to the smell of his father's shaving lotion, to the way the sun shot a dart of light across the floor of his room on bright mornings, and to the springy comfort of the big overstuffed armchair in the living room where he liked to curl up and read. But the Golden Flyer was tearing him away from all that. And Paul felt the tearing like a jagged cut deep inside himself—a cut he didn't know how to bandage.

"Tickets, please." Paul looked up to see the conductor looking expectantly in his direction.

For a few panicky minutes Paul was sure he had lost his ticket, but after fumbling in his wallet, he managed to produce it.

"You've got a long trip ahead of you, son," the conductor said, tearing off part of the long ticket. Returning the rest, he moved on to the next row of seats.

Paul opened up the bag of peanuts that his father had bought for him and began to eat slowly, trying to hold back the questions which flooded into his mind. When would he see his father again? Would he like Aunt Edith and Uncle Harold? Suppose he didn't, could he come back to live with his father?

"Well! I made it!" A stout, gray-haired lady plumped down in the aisle seat next to Paul. "I could just see this train pulling out with me not on it. It's a wonder I didn't have a heart attack running down the platform like that. I wish I'd taken a cab to the station. But Mildred said, 'No, no, you let me take you.' Well, I'll never do that again. I had my bags all packed, all ready to go, and I'm standing around waiting for her. I never saw the beat of that sister of mine. She'll be late for her own funeral."

19

The woman stood up, took off her coat, and folded it neatly so the lining was on the outside. Paul could see that she wanted to store it on the overhead rack, but she was too short to reach it.

"I can put that up for you," he volunteered. "I'll have to stand on the seat, but I guess that won't matter."

"What a nice young man you are. Thank you."

"I can't manage your suitcase, though."

"Don't worry about that. One of the trainmen will put it up when he comes through. I've got my toothbrush in my pocketbook. There's nothing worse than having to drag down your suitcase for every little thing. I remember one trip I was on. I guess it was the time I went to Denver, or maybe it was the summer Mildred and I went East . . ."

Paul smiled at this woman in her bright-green dress. She seemed like the type who would make a batch of fudge and bring you some of it. But he didn't want to listen to her stories. Every once in a while she would pause for breath and he would mumble "Um" or "Uh-huh" as he chewed his peanuts. She really didn't seem to expect him to answer. That was fine with him. He could think his own thoughts and let her ramble on all she wanted to.

Paul finished his peanuts and picked up his magazine, slowly turning the pages. He wondered if he could politely read while Mrs. Green Dress was chattering on and on.

"Are you going to visit your grandmother?"

With a jolt, Paul realized that Mrs. Green Dress was waiting for an answer. "Uh, no. My aunt and

20

uncle." He jerked his head back to get his unruly straw-colored hair out of his eyes. Was Mrs. Green Dress going to start asking him personal questions?

"Do they live in San Francisco?" Again, a pause. He had to answer.

"No . . . in Oakland." He felt himself tense like an animal—listening, assessing the danger, getting ready to spring under cover.

"Most schools don't have a vacation at this time in January."

"No." Could he let it go at that?

"Of course when you travel during the holidays, it's a madhouse. The trains are jammed. I told my daughter I'd come to see her *after* Christmas this year. Last year I must have waited in line for an hour every time I wanted to get into the dining car to eat. Of course this year is different, anyway. Lyda's expecting her new baby any day now, and I've got to be there to take care of her little girl. She's so cute, that granddaughter of mine . . ."

And she was off again. Paul relaxed a little. But he decided that, polite or not, he was going to read. He had no intention of spilling out his whole life story to someone he had known for only a few minutes. Mrs. Green Dress stopped talking before long and started to knit.

After a while a trainman brought pillows and blankets for the passengers. He dimmed the ceiling lights, and the various conversations in the car gradually quieted. Mrs. Green Dress yawned and put away her knitting.

Paul turned off the little reading light above his

seat, lowered the shade at the window, tilted his seat back as far as it would go, and settled down for the night.

The jiggling, jouncing, vibrating motion of the train lulled him to sleep, and all the events of the day became scrambled together in his mind. He thought he was walking through a train station trying to find his father, a station with long, dark corridors and stairways that never seemed to lead to anything but more corridors and stairways. He had lost all his clothes, but the people around him had theirs and yet they didn't pay any attention to his nakedness. Mrs. Green Dress was selling candy, standing behind an impossibly high counter. He could see chocolate bars in crisp paper wrappers mounded up all over the counter. But he couldn't buy one because he couldn't reach up high enough to give her his money.

Sometime in the night he heard the conductor call, "O-ma-ha. This stop is Omaha." Then he fell into a deep sleep and didn't wake up until morning.

3

"Does Your Train Stop in East Broccoli?"

WHEN PAUL PUSHED UP the window shade the next day, he looked out on a dreary landscape. An overcast sky hung low over the frozen prairie. He checked his watch and timetable and calculated that the Flyer must now be speeding across western Nebraska, headed for Cheyenne, Wyoming.

What was his father doing now? Paul pictured him moving around their apartment, frying his eggs and bacon—"Gently now, we're not making shoe leather"—and pouring his coffee. Does he miss me the way I miss him? Paul wondered.

The other passengers began to stir. Paul pulled the lever on the side of his chair and jerked himself into a sitting position.

Mrs. Green Dress looked over at him. "I hope the weather is clear when we get to the mountains. Be prepared to see some gorgeous scenery. You'll have a lot to tell your aunt and uncle when you get to Oakland. Are they going to meet you at the station?"

"They said they would." Paul began to feel uneasy again. Would Mrs. Green Dress ask him why he was

23

traveling alone, why his mother hadn't come with him? How could he answer her? Just blurt out the truth: My mother died of cancer six weeks ago, just before Christmas?

A lump rose in Paul's throat that threatened to strangle him. "Excuse me," he mumbled, stepping over Mrs. Green Dress into the aisle. He wasn't sure what he was going to do next, but he knew he couldn't sit still and answer any more questions.

He walked toward the rear of his coach, concentrating on nothing but getting away—from Mrs. Green Dress, from the tears that he felt welling up.

When he opened the door into the vestibule, the noise of the train was deafening. He felt uneasy crossing the space where his car was connected to the next, because the metal plates shifted under his feet when he stepped on them. What a relief when the door into the next coach closed behind him!

Now the roar of the train was softened, and the floor felt solid under his feet again. He walked quickly up the aisle. But walking on a moving train wasn't easy. Every time the train swayed or lurched, he was thrown off balance.

Maybe one of these unexpected motions caused it, or maybe he wasn't looking where he was going, but Paul found himself slamming into a dark-haired girl who was standing by the water fountain, drinking from a paper cup.

"Hey!" she yelled, wiping away the water that had splashed over her face and down her blouse.

"I didn't see you. I'm sorry."

"Honestly!" The girl gave him a disgusted look and Paul quickly moved on.

In the next car the smell of fresh coffee and frying bacon greeted him and pushed everything out of his mind except breakfast. Tables for four were lined up on both sides of the aisle which led to a stainless steel kitchen. Paul glimpsed cooks in white suits and hats. He guessed this must be the coffee shop car his father had told him about, where the meals were cheaper than in the diner.

Paul sat down in a chair next to the window and ordered corn muffins, bacon, and cocoa.

The white-coated waiter smiled when he brought them and said, "That'll put hair on your chest, son."

The motion of the train made the cocoa jiggle in the cup, and a few drops splashed onto Paul's arm. But the rich chocolate smell and the warm sweetness flowing down his throat as he drank it were comforting, and Paul began to think his trip wasn't so bad after all.

His breakfast finished, he continued his tour of the train. The aisle of the coffee shop made a jog around the kitchen and turned into a narrow passageway that led to the next car, which was the diner. This was like a fancy restaurant, each table draped with a clean, white cloth and decorated with a vase holding a single red rose. Paul knew he would feel very grand if he could eat in there. He imagined himself regally ordering, "Roast falcon, please. And don't forget the parsnip dressing."

Next came the club car, which was a lounge with

a bar for serving drinks at one end. It had sofas and easy chairs arranged with their backs to the windows of the train. Little round tables stood in front of some of the seats. Two tables, like those in the coffee shop, had seats on each side so that four people could sit together.

Following the club car was a bedroom car, which had a long, narrow corridor running down one side of it. The bedrooms were behind stainless steel doors. The train made a sudden lurch, and Paul, to steady himself, grabbed one of the metal bars that stretched across each window.

Then came a pullman car, where some of the seats were still made up into upper and lower berths for sleeping. Striding down the aisle, Paul squared his shoulders and pretended he was decked out in a blue uniform with brass buttons and a shiny brass plate on his cap that said CONDUCTOR in block letters.

"Stillistaka," he muttered under his breath. "The next stop is Stillistaka. This way out. Watch your step, lady."

"Does your train stop in East Broccoli?" asked a deep voice.

Startled, Paul looked up to see a burly barrel of a man with red hair and a bushy red mustache grinning at him. Paul stopped for a minute and stared. How could anyone have heard what he was saying? But this man must have.

Feeling his face grow hot, Paul hurried into the next car, grateful that it was filled with bedrooms where the passengers were behind the doors of their little compartments. Several more bedroom cars followed. Paul hurried through them, looking straight ahead.

But by the time he reached the observation car on the end of the train, he was interested in looking around again. This car had a few bedrooms in it, but the rear of it was a lounge like the club car. Paul liked the little writing desk and chair, and the side tables, with lamps built into them, that doubled as magazine racks.

The end of the car was curved, and in the center of the curve was an emergency door with a window in it. Paul stood for a long time in front of the window, watching the track that stretched back and back and back, all the way to Chicago.

Then he settled down in one of the comfortable chairs and watched the scenery from the side windows. Now and again, when the track curved, Paul caught a glimpse of the whole train snaking its way westward.

But the bleak, gray day made him feel unbearably lonely, so he pulled a stack of magazines out of the rack and tried to forget himself by concentrating on the brightly colored pages. Still, the morning dragged.

About noon, hunger forced him back to his coach seat. Mrs. Green Dress was nowhere to be seen, at least for the moment. If only he could buy his lunch, he wouldn't have to worry about her coming back to badger him with questions. But he had only enough money to buy two breakfasts and a dinner, with a little left over for emergencies.

His lunch was packed carefully in his suitcase, two

peanut butter and jelly sandwiches, a box of fig new-
tons, an orange, and a small bag of powdered milk.
He had had a big argument with his father about the
milk.

"I'll feel like a jerk sprinkling powdered milk into
my water cup. Besides, what'll I stir it up with?"

"I'll give you a spoon."

"Nobody else on the train is going to be drinking
powdered milk."

"You'd be surprised what people take with them in
lunch bags."

"I won't take it. It tastes terrible."

"You might run out of money for regular milk.
Take it. It could come in handy."

His father had won. He had poured the dry milk
out of its big red and white box into a small brown
paper bag and sealed it with scotch tape. Paul had
dutifully put the bag in his suitcase, but he had no
intention of using it. He would give it to Aunt Edith.
Maybe she could cook with it the way his mother
used to.

"This certainly isn't a pretty day." Mrs. Green
Dress was back. Paul looked out over the desolate
prairie stretching back to low hills and bluffs that
seemed to be pressed down by the leaden sky. The
day certainly wasn't pretty. It was gloomy.

"I'll bet you wish you were home playing in your
backyard."

Paul felt suffocated by her strong perfume.
Couldn't she let him alone and stop questioning him?
People who live in third-floor walk-ups don't have
backyards, he wanted to yell at her.

28

Then he remembered the way his father reacted when people asked him things that were none of their business. Once someone asked him how much money he made. He just laughed and said, "Not enough." Then, quick, he got the person talking about the high cost of everything. Would his father's trick work on Mrs. Green Dress? It was worth a try.

"Does your granddaughter have a backyard to play in?"

"Ellen? Only a little one. Lyda and Tom live in Daly City. I don't know if you know where that is, but it's not far from San Francisco. They have a sweet little pink stucco house. It's going to seem smaller with that new baby . . ."

29

Paul settled back happily in his seat, munching a fig newton. If Mrs. Green Dress asked anything personal, he would just keep distracting her. She prattled on for a while, then turned to her knitting.

His lunch finished, Paul took out a balsa wood plane model which Mrs. Flaherty had given him. He put the glue on the windowsill and arranged the pieces of the plane on the seat beside him. Before long, though, he realized that he needed a flat place to work on. Gathering up the parts, he headed for the club car.

Four people were playing cards at one of the large tables. But the other table was empty. Paul carefully arranged his materials there. Putting the plane together was not easy. Every time the train made an unexpected motion, his hands jiggled and he couldn't get the pieces aligned. But this forced him to concentrate harder and gave him no time to worry about meeting Aunt Edith and Uncle Harold.

The car had a homey atmosphere, with its soft carpeting on the floor and gay, striped curtains at the windows. Some passengers were reading, some chatting. Paul felt almost happy. Then in walked the man with the bushy, red mustache.

He didn't sit down, but came to where Paul was working and stood watching the plane take shape. Paul felt the intentness of his look and tried to keep his own mind fixed on his project. But he kept wondering what the man would say to him. Would he say something about catching Paul pretending to be the conductor? Something about the train's going from

East Broccoli to West Asparagus that would make Paul feel like a two-year-old?

But the man said, "That's quite a plane you've got there—Bristol Scout D. They used those in World War I, you know, in the early part of the war."

Paul got up the courage to look the man in the face. Clear-blue eyes met his, eyes that looked straight at him, but with kindness.

"Those planes only flew 100 miles an hour. That's about the speed of this streamliner when it's going full tilt. When you get that model finished, I'd like to see it." The man moved away and sat down to smoke his pipe in a seat next to a fat man with a shiny bald head.

The gray afternoon melted gradually into evening. Soon Paul settled in his coach seat for what he thought would be his last night on the Flyer. Tomorrow, he told himself, he would be with Aunt Edith and Uncle Harold in their house. His stomach began to churn at the thought. But after a while he fell asleep.

31

4

Trouble on the Hill

WHEN PAUL WOKE UP the next morning, the train was stopped. But where? He checked his watch —7:00. Then he looked at his timetable. The station must be Sacramento, because the Flyer was due there at 6:46.

Paul pushed up the shade. Snow was falling and the wind was blowing furiously. Vivid neon signs glowed on both sides of a street and over the street a huge sign was suspended. As Paul read it, his heart sank. The sign said, RENO, THE BIGGEST LITTLE CITY IN THE WORLD.

The train couldn't still be in Reno. It was supposed to leave there in the middle of the night—at 2:22. But the sign stared back at him and clearly it said Reno.

Two trainmen pushed open the door at the rear of the coach, bringing with them a blast of icy air. They walked quickly up the aisle, one behind the other.

"Looks like a real blizzard. Nothing's moving." Paul heard one of them say.

"When do you figure we'll pull out of here?"

"Hard to say. They're cleaning up the slides ahead."

"We'll be lucky if we make it over the Hill. They were stalled yesterday, you know."

Paul felt a vague uneasiness as he watched the men, their coats and flat-topped hats covered with snow, open the door at the front of his coach. Another icy blast and they were gone.

What were the slides that needed cleaning up? Where was "the Hill"? Who was stalled yesterday?

Paul had eaten his breakfast in the coffee shop and returned to his coach seat before the Flyer started moving again. It was running six hours late now. Would Aunt Edith and Uncle Harold wait all those extra hours at the station in Oakland? If they went home, how would they know when to come back to pick him up?

After the train left Reno, it crossed into California, climbing steadily into the Sierra Nevada Mountains. Paul knew he wouldn't be able to see much from the observation car, but curiosity led him there anyway.

He was right. Only the fuzzy outlines of nearby evergreen trees were visible above the drifts piled high on both sides of the track and steadily mounting higher.

"Mind if I join you?" asked a deep voice.

Paul looked up to see the man with the bushy red mustache easing himself into the chair beside him.

"You know," the man began, "it's always snowing in the Sierra. Seems that way, anyway. Once I came here in October to ski, and some years I've skied right up till May. I hope to get some skiing in this year on my way back from the Coast."

The man paused and reached into the pocket of his jacket for his pipe. He filled it carefully from a small leather pouch and lighted it. "The snow is good for skiers. But it's a devil for the railroad."

Paul decided he liked this big, friendly man. "What's the Hill? I heard some trainmen saying they weren't sure we'd make it over the Hill."

"We're on the Hill right now. It's the part of this run between Sparks, Nevada, and Roseville, California—across the Sierra Nevada Mountains. Gorgeous country, but treacherous. The trains couldn't operate on the Hill without their rotaries."

"Rotaries?"

"You know what one of those big window fans looks like?"

Paul nodded.

"Well, just imagine one of them stuck on the front of a locomotive. Only of course it's much bigger. Enormous blades whirl around to cut through the deepest drifts. A fleet of rotaries churn up and down the mountains all through the snow season to keep the rails clear." He drew deeply on his pipe.

Paul decided he had better get answers to more of his questions. "What's a slide? The trainmen said someone was stalled in one yesterday."

"I suspect that someone was yesterday's train. Snowslides are a big danger this time of year. Snow builds up on the sides of the mountains until it can't build up any longer. Then tons of it roar down the mountain, burying everything."

34

Would a snowslide bury the Flyer? Paul shuddered at the thought.

"That's why the railroads need the rotaries. A rotary can clean up a slide in no time, unless the slide lands on top of the rotary." The man must have sensed the fear that began to rise in Paul because he added, "But that very rarely happens."

Suddenly, the whiteness of the falling snow was blocked out and Paul felt darkness closing over the train. Without thinking, he ducked and covered his head with his hands as if to ward off the impact of the snow that he expected to crush down on the Flyer any second.

The man touched his arm gently and said, "This is another way the railroad protects the trains."

Paul raised his head and looked out. He smiled at himself when he saw that the train was inside a tall wooden tunnel. The boards that formed it had narrow spaces between them where snow sifted through, but the tunnel protected the train from the worst of the storm.

The Flyer stopped.

"Only about four miles of these snowsheds are left. When the track was first laid, the railroad built about forty miles of them. But a lot of sheds were torn down because they blocked out the beautiful scenery. And some of them burned down."

When the Flyer eased out of the snowshed, Paul looked at his watch—11:23. The train was now seven hours late. It moved forward slowly on more shed-protected track and then headed out into the howling storm. The red and green signal lights looked startlingly brilliant against the white snow. The Flyer gained speed, but not much.

"See here," the red-mustached man said. "I've been lecturing you for a long time and I haven't introduced myself. I'm Horace Walton."

"I'm Paul Sullivan." Paul liked the feel of Mr. Walton's large, firm hand as he shook it.

The train inched along. Even on a downgrade it moved slowly.

"Are the rotaries out now?" Paul wanted to know.

"You can count on it."

Paul found himself unable to concentrate on anything but the train's progress. Mr. Walton fell silent, too, as if he were also trying mentally to push the streamliner along.

Paul studied his wristwatch. Time seemed to crawl as laboriously as the train. 11:40. 11:42. 11:45. Paul began to feel that noon had some kind of magical significance. If only the Flyer could struggle along until then, it would be safe from the deepening drifts that were piling up on the tracks and from snowslides that could bury it.

Snow swirled viciously around the streamliner. 11:50. 11:53. 11:55. Noon! Now maybe the Flyer would roll down the track safely to Sacramento and on to Oakland.

But the train did not pick up speed. It strained forward, creeping around a ledge that lay open to the full force of the blizzard. And then it stopped. Paul's watch read 12:15.

5

Green-Humped Camels

PAUL STARED out at the snow-shrouded mountain scene. On one side of the Flyer the ground sloped downward. On the other side he could see the eastbound tracks and beyond them the steep cliffs.

Surely he didn't need to worry. The train had stopped earlier and had started again. Yes, Paul thought, but that stop had been inside a snowshed. This one is right in the middle of the storm.

He turned to Mr. Walton for reassurance. "Why are we stopped?"

"I suspect we may have stopped for a snowslide."

"How can we get past it?"

"We can't. We'll probably be backing down the track in a minute."

They looked out into the blizzard and waited. Mr. Walton puffed calmly on his pipe. Paul tried to hear some sound that would tell him the train was beginning to move again. But all he heard was the screeching wind. It felt as if the train were suspended in space, cut off from everything and everyone by a sea of snow.

He sighed noisily. The train would back up in a minute and everything would be all right.

But the Flyer didn't move. Would a snowslide hurtle down the mountainside and bury the train? How could Mr. Walton sit so calmly?

The snow kept falling and falling and falling, and the train remained motionless. Paul rubbed the back of his neck. He sighed again. Then he got up abruptly. "Nice talking to you, Mr. Walton."

"Nice talking to you, too, Paul," Mr. Walton answered.

The Flyer tilted in toward the mountainside, which made walking difficult and gave Paul a weird, off-balance feeling. He kept looking for a trainman who could tell him what was wrong. If he knew exactly what was happening, maybe he would feel better. But no trainman was in sight.

When he came to the coffee shop, he decided to eat. He had no more food in his suitcase, because he hadn't expected to have another lunch on the train. He had trouble finding a seat, but finally he located one across from a thin, white-haired lady.

The lady looked up from the pie she was eating. Her deep-set eyes were friendly. "Well, hello there," she said.

Paul threw back his head to get his hair out of his eyes. "Hi."

"Can I get you something, sonny?" a waiter asked.

With a sinking feeling, Paul realized that he had only five dollars left. If the train were stalled for a long time, he would have to buy dinner too, and that would leave him even less. But he could sense the waiter's impatience, so he had to say something. "I'll have a grilled cheese sandwich and a cup of cocoa."

"Are you enjoying your train trip?" the white-haired lady asked.

"It's fine." Would this lady start asking him personal questions the way Mrs. Green Dress had? Slowly, Paul unclenched his hands and spread his fingers flat on the table. "Do you know why the train is stopped?" He tried to sound casual.

"No, but it'll start moving again before we know it, I expect." The woman smiled, finished up her pie, and left the table.

Her answer wasn't very satisfying. Paul suspected she didn't know much about the danger of snow-slides in the Sierra. Still, she sounded so relaxed and confident that Paul couldn't help feeling comforted.

The food made him feel better, too. It made him remember being at home at the kitchen table with the blue and white checked oilcloth over it. His mother often had made grilled cheese sandwiches. On cold days she had cocoa ready when he came home from school. Only she put a marshmallow on top and this cup had whipped cream.

But now what? The train still wasn't moving, and Paul knew he had to do something to keep himself from worrying about it. He had read all the reading material available. He had put together his model. That left his sketching pad and crayons. Drawing could sometimes absorb his attention for hours. He would soon find out if it would help him now.

He collected his crayons, paper, and scissors from his suitcase in the coach and headed toward the observation car. Today he needed company while he drew.

He recognized two of the people in the observation car. One was the fat, bald man that Mr. Walton had sat beside yesterday and the other was the girl with the dark hair whom he had bumped into. The fat man was puffing on a cigarette. The girl was playing with a paddle-ball, trying to bounce the little red ball which was attached by a rubber string to the wooden paddle. She wasn't very good at it, and she didn't seem interested in it, either, for she kept swinging her legs and looking out of the window.

Paul wondered if she remembered him and if she thought he was stupid for running into her. She looked to be about his age, so he sat down in the empty seat next to her, but he decided not to risk starting a conversation.

He set to work drawing a desert scene. It was the farthest thing away from the unmoving train and the snowstorm that he could think of.

As he drew, the girl watched. After a while, she said, "Do you like to draw?"

"A lot. I like to draw camels with green humps."

The girl stared at him as if he had suddenly sprouted a green hump.

Paul decided to spin as wild a tale as he could invent. "I started drawing them after I took a trip through the Arabian Desert with my parents last year." He smiled, trying to imagine himself on a trip through the Arabian Desert. The only time he had been out of Chicago was when his parents had taken him to Clinton, Iowa, to see his mother's folks. His

40

grandparents had died soon afterward, and he had never been back.

"Say, what's your name?" the girl asked abruptly.

"Paul. What's yours?"

"Kathy. And that's my mother and my baby sister, Betsy. She's seven months old." Kathy motioned with her head toward a small, delicately pretty woman holding a baby.

"Well, anyway," Paul said, anxious to get control of the conversation before Kathy started asking questions about his family. He had a feeling that she couldn't be diverted as easily as Mrs. Green Dress.

But Kathy interrupted. "We're going to San Francisco to be with my father. He's in the Navy and he's stationed out there."

Paul felt a twinge of envy. Did Kathy know how lucky she was to be traveling with her mother and looking forward to seeing her father?

"Well, anyway," he repeated. "The camels that carried us were a very strange breed. Moss backs they call them. No one understands why their humps are covered with green hair instead of the regular camel-colored hair."

Kathy looked doubtful. "Is that really true?"

"Sure. I'd show you pictures of them in my photograph album, but I left it at home. Here, let me draw one for you." Paul sketched a one-humped camel with a vivid green hump. "Hey, I've got a great idea," he said.

He took the scissors out of his pocket and started cutting out the camel.

"What are you doing?" Kathy asked.

41

Paul started drawing another camel. "I'll cut this camel out too. Then we can pretend we're riding them across the desert. We'll be sheiks."

Kathy's face came alive and her eyes began to shine. She yanked off the green scarf that had been tied neatly under the collar of her white blouse and placed it over her head so that it hung down over her face. "I'll be a beautiful Arabian princess who goes with the sheik."

"We own fabulous jewels. We're carrying them across the desert on our moss-backed camels. And there are robbers hiding out, waiting for us so they can steal the jewels." Paul was beginning to enjoy himself.

"And the jewels are magical. There's a golden sapphire—" Kathy said.

"A *golden* sapphire? There's no such thing as a golden sapphire! Sapphires are blue."

"That's what I mean," Kathy went on. "It's the only golden sapphire in existence. And it has magical powers. That's why the robbers are after it."

"Okay." Paul decided he liked Kathy.

She was really wound up now. "The golden sapphire has the power to change ordinary rocks into jewels. You hold the rock in one hand and the golden sapphire in the other and say, 'Omar Romar, Curry Comb' and the plain ordinary rock turns into a jewel —any kind of jewel. You can't have any say over what kind of jewel it becomes."

"I like that," Paul said, smiling. He handed her one of the green-humped camels he had cut out. "Here's your camel. And mine is walking along just ahead of

42

it." He trotted his paper camel across the arm of Kathy's chair.

Paul was pulled back to reality by the sight of something huge and black behind the curtain of snow. He dropped his paper camel and went to the window of the rear emergency door for a better look. Something was definitely approaching on the track behind the streamliner. Whatever it was belched black smoke that mixed with the whirling snow to form thick billowing clouds in a dozen shades of gray.

The fat, bald man was standing beside Paul now, and together they watched as the tender of a steam locomotive emerged, stopping about a car's length and a half behind them.

43

Next, three trainmen began shoveling furiously. They cleared the tracks between the Flyer and the tender, scraped away the snow from the coupler at the end of the streamliner, then jumped to one side. The steam locomotive slowly backed up until it coupled to the Flyer with a jolt and a clanking bang.

"Now they can pull us out of this snowslide!" The fat man took a puff on his cigarette.

So Mr. Walton was right. The Flyer had been stopped by a snowslide. But in a few minutes the train would be moving toward safety. Paul felt his whole body relax. He stared expectantly at the locomotive.

The Flyer made strange creaking noises. But it didn't budge. Snow soon piled up on the couplers again.

"Come on, Paul," Kathy called. "The robbers are getting set to capture our jewels."

Paul paid no attention. He continued to stare ahead, waiting, hypnotized by the steady descent of the snow.

The conductor came into the car and walked to the rear window, standing just behind Paul and the fat man.

"Why aren't we moving?" Paul asked.

"We can't move," the conductor replied.

"Can't move? Why not?"

"We're frozen to the tracks."

6

Will the Train Ever Start Moving?

"I'VE NEVER HEARD of such a thing," the fat man said.

"It's true whether you've heard of it or not," the conductor stated. "The brake rigging, underfloor tanks, everything. Frozen solid."

The fat man ground out his cigarette in the ashtray. "Why is that steam locomotive still coupled up to our train?"

"It's got problems, too. That locomotive is pushing a rotary plow. The air pump on the rotary failed, so the locomotive can't move either."

Paul felt as if the wind had been knocked out of him. What did this mean? Could a train that was frozen to the tracks be thawed out and made to run again? From the looks of the storm, no thaw was likely to come for a long time.

"Isn't there any way we can get out?" Paul asked.

"We'll get another rotary in here soon to plow away the slide in front of the train. Then maybe we can pull it ahead." The conductor looked down at Paul through his steel-rimmed glasses and smiled.

45

"Don't worry, son, we'll get you out of here." Then he turned and left the car.

"Hey, Paul," Kathy called again. "Come on. The robbers are getting set to capture our jewels."

Feeling dazed, Paul moved away from the rear window. He sat down beside Kathy and picked up one of the camels he had cut out. Why did Kathy look and sound so *normal?* She didn't seem to be worried about the train. Maybe if your mother is with you and you're going to be with your dad in a little while, maybe a train being frozen to the tracks doesn't bother you.

Kathy went on as if nothing had happened. "I've got the golden sapphire. I've sewn it into the waistband of my skirt. But all the other jewels are strapped onto the camels' backs." She trotted the camel briskly along the arm of her chair.

Listlessly, Paul moved his camel behind Kathy's. Then he handed it to her. "You can have this," he said. "I don't feel like playing Arabs anymore."

Paul carefully replaced his crayons in their box, put his scissors in his pocket, tucked his sketching pad under his arm, and left the car.

He couldn't bear to sit still. He had to be up and moving, to figure things out. Aunt Edith and Uncle Harold bothered him most. They would be waiting in the station in Oakland to pick him up. Or would they? Had they gone back to their house?

He threw his head back to flip his hair out of his eyes and pushed open the door to one of the bedroom cars.

He headed down the corridor while the wind

screamed outside like a banshee. He had heard that sound before, in horror movies, and it made the skin on his arms prickle.

A sudden roar blotted out the scream. Startled, Paul jumped. A passenger train that looked like a twin of the Flyer slid smoothly past, its windows brightly lighted.

Paul laughed and waved when he saw a boy about his age looking out of a window at him. The boy smiled and waved back. Each table in the diner was decorated with a vase holding a single rose. While the streamliner was passing, Paul felt that the Flyer was moving again. But then the other train was gone, and he realized that the Flyer was still motionless.

Paul wanted to yell, Wait! Wait for me! Take me with you. The corridor seemed unbearably silent and empty, and the slant of it was annoying.

Another problem popped into his mind. If the train was stuck much longer, he would have to eat another meal on the train. This meant spending more of his money. If he had to buy food, how would he have enough to get to Aunt Edith's house? Tomorrow would be Monday, a workday for Uncle Harold. Aunt Edith might not be able to drive to the station to pick him up. A cab would be awfully expensive. Even a bus might cost a lot—if buses ran past their house.

At home if he felt this mixed up about something, he could put on his hat and coat and take a long walk. But with the snow blowing the drifts deeper and deeper around the Golden Flyer, he was trapped.

Back in his coach seat, Paul tried drawing again. He made pictures of elephants with cats' heads and butterflies with elephants' heads. He was grateful that Mrs. Green Dress wasn't around to ask questions.

The storm was bringing the day to an early end. When he looked out of the window now, all he saw was his own face staring back at him.

The problem of dinner couldn't be ignored much longer. Paul pulled out his wallet and studied its contents. He had a little over four dollars left. He promised himself he would spend no more than a dollar.

The coffee shop seemed cozy, filled with the sounds of pleasant chatter. The ceiling lights cast a warm glow over the tables. Paul ordered another grilled cheese sandwich and a cup of cocoa. It didn't fill him up, but it stopped his stomach from growling, and he walked back to his seat, feeling sleepy.

Mrs. Green Dress looked up from her knitting with a welcoming smile. This is sort of like coming home, Paul thought, silently chuckling at the idea.

He pushed the lever on the side of his seat so that his chair tilted back as far as it would go. Then he arranged his blanket over him and snuggled his head into his pillow. "I think I'll try to go to sleep now," he said.

"Good idea," Mrs. Green Dress told him. "I'm not going to knit much longer. I'm tired too."

Paul liked the clicking of her knitting needles. It was a comforting, homey sound. His mother had liked to knit. He started to drift off to sleep.

Men's voices under his window roused him. Sitting up, Paul cupped his hands around his face so that he could see out. Through the furiously blowing snow he saw track workers starting to shovel away the snow that was piled halfway up the side of the car. One of the men caught sight of him and waved. Paul waved back.

"What's happening out there?" Mrs. Green Dress wanted to know.

"Some men have come to shovel us out," Paul said. He pulled the window shade down and lay back in his seat again.

"I expect they'll have us shoveled out before long," Mrs. Green Dress said without looking up from her knitting.

"I guess so." Paul shut his eyes, but he could no

longer shut out his worries. He could see again the conductor staring out of the rear window of the observation car saying, *We're frozen to the tracks. . . . The brake rigging, underfloor tanks, everything. Frozen solid.* Did Mrs. Green Dress know about that? What if the men did shovel the snow from around the train, what good would it do? What had happened to the rotary that was supposed to plow away the snow in front of the train?

Paul felt a stab of fear. If only he weren't alone, if only he could talk to his dad. Mr. Walton! He could talk to Mr. Walton! He knew all about trains, he would know what was going on. First thing in the morning he would look him up. Gradually, Paul's muscles relaxed and he fell asleep.

When he woke at daylight, most of the other passengers, including Mrs. Green Dress, were still sleeping. He pushed the lever on his chair so that the back moved to an upright position, then he pushed up the window shade. His heart sank. He couldn't even see where the men had shoveled. Snow was still coming down fast, and it had drifted almost level with the windowsill. Paul pulled the shade down again.

His empty stomach had an ominous feel to it. He would have to spend more to fill it up—for breakfast and probably for lunch. He didn't dare think beyond that. He would spend as little as he could get away with and hope for the best.

And he had to find Mr. Walton, but that shouldn't be too difficult. If he walked through the train, he would be sure to run into him. After all, where could he go?

Paul set out for the coffee shop, and luck was with him. Mr. Walton was sitting alone at one of the tables.

"Hello there, Paul," Mr. Walton said heartily. "I'm glad to see you again. Come, join me, unless you're waiting for someone."

"No, I'm not waiting for anyone."

"Come, then, let me treat you to breakfast. I never like to eat alone."

Paul sat down, trying not to show how grateful he was. If Mr. Walton paid for this meal, he could stretch his money a little further. Just the same, he felt embarrassed.

Paul was drinking his second cup of cocoa when the conductor led the track workers into the car. "You can thaw out here and get some hot food in your stomachs," the conductor said.

Red-faced and snow-covered, the men stamped in and sank into the vacant chairs. Snow melted in muddy rivers from their boots. The crystals that clung to their hair and eyebrows were soon running down their cheeks like tears.

"Gentlemen, we salute you!" Mr. Walton announced grandly. He stood up and began to clap. Then another table rose and joined in the clapping, and another table—until all the passengers were on their feet. The workers' tired faces broke into grins.

"You fellas worked like crazy out there all night long!" one passenger said. "Did you make any headway?"

A stocky worker shook his head. "We made a passageway to the baggage car and we're trying to keep one window in each car shoveled off." He took a long

51

drink from his coffee cup.

Mr. Walton turned to the conductor. "Did that rotary ever get in here and plow out the slide in front of the train?"

"Yes, they had no trouble doing that, but a slide fell behind them and trapped them." The conductor adjusted his glasses.

"Why couldn't they just back up?" Paul asked.

"Don't you see, the rotary plow was facing toward the Flyer. If it had backed up, the locomotive that was pushing it would have gotten jammed in the snowdrifts," the conductor explained patiently.

Mr. Walton stroked the ends of his mustache thoughtfully. "How are you planning to get us out now?"

"The track we're on is blocked with snow and buried equipment. There's a chance we can get a relief train to come on the eastbound track and pick us up. But we've got to keep the track open. And that's no easy job with the snow falling as fast as it is and the wind blowing like a hurricane. A locomotive with a rotary plow attached to each end is on its way right now. So maybe we'll be out of here before too long."

The conductor moved to the tables where the exhausted track workers were hunched over their breakfast. "More coffee, fellas?" he asked.

Paul leaned across the table toward Mr. Walton. "How long do you think we'll be stuck here?" he asked.

"Hard to tell. This storm is a bad one."

"If they've got a locomotive coming with a rotary

plow hitched onto each end, that means it can't get stuck, right?"

"That's the idea, yes."

"If a snowslide comes roaring down the mountain in front of it, the plow can roar right through it." Paul looked at Mr. Walton for confirmation.

Mr. Walton nodded.

"And if a snowslide comes tearing down the mountain in back of it, the plow can back up and clear that away, too."

"Right."

"So there's nothing to worry about."

"Let's hope so." Mr. Walton smiled.

But his eyes aren't smiling, Paul thought. He doesn't look that certain. "What's a relief train?" Paul asked.

"Well, I'll tell you one thing, it'll be a relief to see it." Mr. Walton chuckled and reached into his pocket for his pipe. He didn't light it, he just held it in his mouth and sucked on it. Every once in a while he took it out to gesture with. "You see, the railroad has sent, or it will send, a special train to get us. It'll be a train like this one, except that it won't be a streamliner that's on the printed schedules. It's just for us."

"It'll get here soon, won't it?"

"As soon as it can in this blizzard."

Abruptly, Paul turned to another problem that was bothering him. "Say, my aunt and uncle are supposed to meet me in Oakland. Do you think they know something's happened to the train?"

"I'm sure they know. They'll call the railroad sta-

53

tion and find out when the Flyer is expected in." Mr. Walton looked directly at Paul with his clear, blue eyes. He didn't seem in any hurry to leave the table.

Paul wanted to be reassured even more, but he couldn't think of words to capture his uneasiness. He got up hurriedly. "I—thank you very much for the breakfast."

"Thank you for your company," Mr. Walton replied.

Paul headed toward the observation car, going over in his mind all that the conductor and Mr. Walton had said, telling himself that the relief train would get through before long.

7

Mr. Walton's Plan

"SEEN ANY MOSS-BACKED CAMELS LATELY?"
Paul looked around to see where the voice came
from. Kathy, the girl he had talked to the day before,
was sitting in an easy chair in the club car. Her
mother and baby sister were sitting nearby on a small
sofa.

Kathy grinned. "Are you going to draw some more
camels today?"

·Paul brushed the hair out of his eyes. "I don't
know."

"I'm going to keep the ones you gave me. They're
really nice. Do you take drawing lessons?"

"No, but I've always liked to draw. Say, are you
going to stay here for a while?"

"I guess so."

"I've got an idea. I'll be right back." Paul returned
a few minutes later with his crayons and sketching
pad. He sat down next to Kathy, spread his pad on his
lap, and laid his crayons on the seat beside him. He
stared intently at Kathy's face.

Kathy began to fidget. "Why are you staring at me?"

Paul squinted as he held a crayon at arm's length. "I'm going to draw a picture of you. I'm trying to get the proportions right for your face."

"Why don't you draw some more camels?" Kathy asked.

Kathy's mother looked up from feeding Betsy her bottle. "Why, Kathy," she said. "Don't you want a picture of yourself?"

"Not like this. If you want a picture of me, Paul, I'm not going to be plain, old Kathy Cummings. I'm going to be the Princess with the Golden Sapphire." She hurried out of the car. When she returned she had a long blue chiffon scarf. "Mama, can I borrow your dangly earrings and that pin you have with the gold-colored stone in it?"

"Oh, Kathy, I don't see why you can't be your own sweet self."

"Because my own sweet self isn't exciting enough, Mama. Please can I borrow the earrings and the pin? Just for the picture?"

Mrs. Cummings sighed. "Oh dear, I suppose so. You'll have to get them. They're in my purse."

Kathy tipped her head back and pulled her long hair away from her face. Then she snapped on the earrings. She fastened the pin through several thicknesses of the chiffon, then arranged the scarf on her head with the pin just above her forehead. "Now you can draw my picture," she announced.

Paul set to work at once. The world of stalled trains and blizzards disappeared from his mind as he strug-

56

gled to create a likeness of Kathy on his paper.

Outside the train the storm continued to rage. Snow had inched above the windowsill now, but Paul was unaware of it. He finished Kathy's picture and handed it to her.

She held it at arm's length for a few minutes, studying it carefully. Then she brought it close to her and exclaimed, "I love it, Paul. I really love it."

Paul drew a lot of other things to amuse Kathy, like flowerpots with wings, flying after geraniums. He began to feel cold but didn't think too much about it. The morning slipped by pleasantly.

"I think we'd better have lunch, children," Mrs. Cummings said finally. "Paul, won't you come to the coffee shop with us?"

Paul agreed. He wondered, though, if he could stand another meal of grilled cheese and cocoa. But that combination was about all he could afford because his money was disappearing so fast.

Once in the coffee shop, he got a welcome surprise. The steward announced that lunch was on the house. Paul couldn't help smiling when he realized that he didn't need to worry so much about using up his money. He barely noticed that lunch was skimpy or that the train was getting colder. Being with Kathy and her family made him feel as if he had a family again. For a while he forgot his loneliness.

His good feelings didn't last long, though. Kathy agreed to take care of Betsy while her mother rested, so Paul headed back to his own coach seat.

Walking through the train, he began to notice an uneasiness in the passengers. Only a little while before, people had seemed relaxed—chatting, reading, or resting. Now he sensed a tension. He noticed that people were bundling up in coats and looking anxiously at the snow, which was definitely above the windowsills now.

When he reached his seat, he saw that Mrs. Green Dress was wearing her navy-blue coat with the gray fur collar. She was knitting more determinedly than usual and her cheeriness had disappeared.

"Oh, hello there," she said. "I thought you'd be back before long to get your coat."

Paul sat down, trying to figure out what was going on. Now that he thought about it, he was getting uncomfortably cold. He stood up on his seat and yanked his coat off the overhead rack. He didn't want to ask Mrs. Green Dress any questions. She had a way of never stopping once she started talking. Maybe, if he was quiet and patient, she would mention what was going on.

But Mrs. Green Dress sat tight-lipped, knitting grimly. Paul looked around at the other people in the car. No one was saying much, but he caught a scrap of conversation.

". . . since the train ran out of fuel."

Out of what? Fuel. Paul was sure that was what the man had said. No wonder the train was getting cold. Where was that relief train?

Paul reached for his drawing pad and crayons. Then he remembered that he had left them in the club car. He had to get them. He couldn't just sit still waiting to freeze.

But when he reached the club car, he forgot about his pad and crayons. An angry crowd was gathered around the tables.

"Why can't someone do something to get us out of this mess?" a sailor was saying.

Paul looked the crowd over. He recognized Mr. Walton sitting with his back to a window, drumming his fingers softly on the arm of his chair. He was dressed warmly in a heavy ski parka, ski pants, and ski boots. The fat man was there, too, standing in the aisle. Kathy and her mother and baby sister were sitting near the door. Kathy was wearing a woolen coat and Betsy was wrapped snugly in blankets.

Paul slipped into an empty chair beside Kathy.

"I'd feel better if I thought the railroad officials really knew how bad things are for us," the sailor continued.

"Just answer me this. Just answer me this. You tell me why they let that streamliner go by yesterday," the fat man demanded.

"They're sending a relief train. The conductor told us that this morning," Mr. Walton said.

"How is the relief train going to get here?" the fat man asked.

Mr. Walton explained. "The conductor said that a locomotive with a rotary plow attached to each end—"

"I guess you haven't heard," the fat man interrupted.

Paul felt the muscles in his stomach tighten.

"Heard what?" Mr. Walton asked.

"This railroad. They've got lots of swell ideas. Trouble is, none of them work," the fat man went on.

60

Mr. Walton leaned forward. "I don't know what you're talking about."

"That locomotive with the rotaries. That's what I'm talking about. Nothing could stop it, right?" The fat man's voice was getting louder.

"Right."

"Well, an avalanche stopped it!"

"An avalanche?" Paul asked, not wanting to believe what the fat man had said.

"Yeah, an avalanche. The driver of one of the rotaries was killed. A tidal wave of snow roared down the mountainside, turned over his plow, and buried it." The fat man paused. No one spoke.

Paul's heart was beating so loudly that he wondered if Kathy could hear it. Mr. Walton must have been afraid something like this would happen. That's why he hadn't been too reassuring this morning, Paul thought.

The fat man went on, his voice becoming louder and more insistent. "Now answer me this. How are we going to get out of here with both tracks blocked?"

"How did you find all this out?" Mr. Walton asked.

"One of the track workers told me. I make it my business to know what's going on. Things are going from bad to worse around here."

"What if one of us gets sick or injured? What will happen to us way off here in the middle of nowhere?" a thin lady with white hair asked. Paul recognized her as the woman he had sat with in the coffee shop yesterday.

"There's a doctor on board," Mr. Walton said.

61

"Nice chap. I met him this morning. He's on his way to Hawaii for a vacation."

"I feel better knowing we have a doctor with us," the white-haired lady said. "But how do we know an avalanche isn't going to bury us the way it buried those plows?"

"We don't know. We just hope and pray," Mr. Walton said.

"Hope! A lot of good that'll do us. We need help!" the fat man shouted.

"There's not much we can do but wait until help can get to us," the white-haired lady said.

"That's what I hate." Mr. Walton's voice was intense. "I hate this sitting around, not being able to do anything."

Paul bit his thumbnail and stared across the aisle at the blue and red stripes in the curtains. He didn't dare look into anyone's eyes.

"If I thought those railroad guys were really trying, I could wait more patiently," the fat man said.

"It's the cold that's got me worried," the sailor said. "I wonder how long we can stay here like this without freezing to death."

"It's my baby I'm concerned about." Mrs. Cummings' voice was soft but insistent. "There's no more milk for her. I don't know what I'll do when she gets hungry again."

"And what will the rest of us do? There's no more grub left for anyone. The dining car steward admitted it!" the fat man exclaimed.

Mr. Walton slammed his hand down hard on the

arm of his chair. "That settles it. I'm going."

The words hit Paul like a slap.

"Going?" several people asked at once.

"To the nearest railroad phone. There must be one not too far up the tracks."

"But it may be miles away," the sailor said.

"Miles away through snow up to your neck," the fat man added.

"I wouldn't go in weather like this," the white-haired lady advised.

"You could easily be lost in this blizzard," the sailor warned. "And you might never be found again—alive."

Paul felt weak and tired and confused. Mr. Walton might be able to help by getting to a phone, but if he were lost . . .

"I'm not a stranger to hiking under difficult conditions and I know this part of the Sierra. I can't sit here any longer. If I go now, I ought to be able to make it back by dark." Mr. Walton sounded calm and confident.

"You going to walk?" the fat man asked.

"I have skis in the baggage car."

"Suppose you do get to a phone, what good will it do?"

"I can talk to the railroad officials and find out what's happening."

"They'll just tell you what the conductor tells us."

"I can also send telegrams to the President and the senators from Nevada and California to make sure they know what's going on here. They ought to be able to get help for us. Wish me luck!" Mr. Walton pulled on his ski gloves and waved almost gaily as he left the car.

The fat man shook his head. "He's out of his mind. He'll never make it."

Paul wasn't so sure.

8

Paul Thinks of a Way

THE PASSENGERS in the club car seemed stunned after Mr. Walton left. Paul just sat still staring at the door, a mixture of hope and dread in his heart. Mr. Walton had said he was an experienced skier. He had said he knew this part of the country. Paul felt that if anyone could get to a phone and back again, Mr. Walton could. But could *anyone* get through this storm safely?

"Why don't you draw some pictures, Paul?" Kathy's voice startled him.

"Uh, I guess I just don't feel like drawing now. I think I'll go back to my seat." Paul found his crayons and paper on the chair where he had left them. He picked them up and started walking in the direction of his coach car.

But when he reached his seat, he had no desire to sit down, so he left his drawing supplies there and kept walking up the aisle. At the front of the car, he stopped for a drink of water at the fountain. He pulled a white triangular cup out of the slot, held it under the spigot, and pushed the metal button. But nothing happened. He pushed the button again. Still nothing.

A man walking by looked at him sympathetically. "There's no more water, son," he said.

No water? Paul's legs felt suddenly weak. No heat. No food. And now, no water.

Paul opened the door into the vestibule. The car ahead was the baggage car. He knew passengers weren't supposed to go in it, but Mr. Walton must have gone in to get his skis. Maybe he was still there.

Paul moved ahead into the dark baggage car. It was piercingly cold and had no light except for what little came in from the partially opened sliding door on the side. Paul could see the vague outlines of trunks and suitcases.

"Mr. Walton?"

No answer. Paul took a few steps forward, tripped over a box, and went sprawling headfirst onto the grimy floor.

"Mr. Walton?" he called again. Only the howl of the wind outside answered him.

Paul got to his feet and groped his way toward the outside door. Snow blew into his face and cold bit into his cheeks. He clenched his hands and drew them up under the sleeves of his coat. As he stood in the doorway, squinting into the storm, a track worker caught sight of him.

"Where you going, sonny?" the man yelled, moving closer.

Paul had no answer.

"This is no weather for you to be out in. You go back inside and try to keep warm."

Feeling foolish, Paul turned around and walked back into the train. He headed for the club car.

Kathy and her mother were still there. Betsy had wakened and had begun to whimper.

Paul had no sooner sat down with them than the conductor approached Kathy's mother and put his hand gently on her shoulder. "Mrs. Cummings, we're moving you from the coach into a bedroom," he told her. "I think you and your children will be more comfortable there."

Mrs. Cummings looked surprised. "I thought the bedroom cars were all filled."

"They were. But that stout gentleman who was in here a while ago has given up his room."

"The fat, bald one?" Kathy asked.

The conductor smiled. "That's the one."

"How nice of him," Mrs. Cummings said. "But where will he sleep now?"

"He'll go into one of the coaches."

Mrs. Cummings smiled thoughtfully. Suddenly Betsy's whimper changed to a cry and Mrs. Cummings' expression changed immediately. "Sir, I wonder, is there just a little milk for my baby?"

The conductor shook his head. "I'm afraid not. You've probably found out there isn't any water left either. We hope to get some food before night, though. Come, I'll show you to your bedroom."

Mrs. Cummings held Betsy tightly in her arms as she and Kathy followed the conductor out of the car.

Paul wanted to follow them to find out where their new room was, but he didn't want to make a pest of himself. After all, he didn't belong to Kathy's family.

He didn't belong to anyone right now. He sat at the empty table pretending to look out of the window. But his eyes were squeezed shut. He didn't dare turn around for a long while.

The light in the car was very dim. No wonder, Paul thought, noticing that the snow was continuing to creep up the window. He sat shivering in the cold car, wishing he could go home. Why had his father thought sending him to California was such a good idea?

The white-haired lady was still sitting in the same chair she had been sitting in when Mr. Walton left. Paul stared at her, remembering how worried her voice sounded when she told Mr. Walton not to go out into the storm. She looked up. "It's awfully dark in here," she said. "Can't the lights be turned on?"

Paul glanced at the ceiling. The lights were off.

A woman in a purple coat, pacing up and down the aisle, stopped beside the older woman. "We have no more electricity, you know," she said gently.

No more lights? Paul felt as if his stomach was one hard knot. More and more he wished he was at home. Out of this. If help didn't come soon, what would happen?

The Golden Flyer was beginning to feel like a refrigerator. The cold from the floor passed right through his shoes. Paul noticed that his hands were clenched and his heart was beating rapidly.

He couldn't sit still any longer. He had to move around and he had to get on warmer clothes.

He found heavy socks in his suitcase. One pair he pulled on over his shoes. Another he tied around his ankles. He took off his coat, pulled on a sweatshirt, a sweater, and a second pair of trousers, then put his coat back on. His wool cap felt good on his head, and his hands were warmer inside his mittens.

Next he decided to try to find Kathy. But how could he find her? He couldn't go knocking on all the bedroom doors asking if Kathy was there.

He headed toward the back of the train. Maybe if he walked through the bedroom cars he would just happen to see Kathy coming out of her room. Or maybe her door would be open.

Paul looked straight ahead, trying to avoid seeing the grim looks on the passengers' faces, as he walked through the cars. He was relieved to reach the bedroom cars. But he still didn't know how to find Kathy. Each small bedroom door was shut tight.

He had just about decided to sit in the observation car for a while, when he heard a baby crying. That had to be Betsy. Mrs. Cummings had asked the conductor for milk and Betsy had been crying when she left the club car. She was crying so loud now that she must really need her milk.

Milk! Paul stopped in the middle of the corridor and began to smile. Of course! Why hadn't he thought of it before? He didn't have to feel like a trapped animal. He had a job to do—and an important one.

9

One Less Hungry Passenger

HE TURNED AROUND and headed back to his coach. He found his brown paper lunch bag squashed under his seat and opened it eagerly. But his heart sank. It was empty.

Then he remembered. He had put the bag of powdered milk in his suitcase. He found it in one of the side pockets, pulled it out, snapped the case shut again, and hurried back in the direction of Kathy's car.

Good grief. He had forgotten. No water. The powdered milk wasn't such a great idea after all. Yes, it was. At the very least it was a reason for knocking on Kathy's door. But what if the baby had stopped crying?

Paul need not have worried. The baby's cries sounded even more desperate than they had earlier. Kathy answered Paul's knock. Mrs. Cummings was rocking the baby back and forth in her arms.

"I have some powdered milk. Could you use that for the baby?" Paul asked.

The frantic look vanished from Mrs. Cummings'

face. "Oh, Paul! Yes! You wonderful boy. How did you happen to find it?"

"I had it in my bag. But what can we use for water?"

Mrs. Cummings' face clouded.

"Snow!" Kathy yelled.

"Yes, dear," her mother said patiently. "But how do we melt it with no fuel on the train?"

"First we'll get the snow, then we'll ask the people in the kitchen to help us," Paul suggested.

Betsy's face was bright red now. She angrily spit out the pacifier that Mrs. Cummings tried to put in her mouth.

"Children, take the bottle and the milk to the conductor and see if he can help you. And hurry."

Outside in the corridor, Paul and Kathy tried to decide how to proceed. "We'll waste a lot of time if we try to find the conductor first," Paul said. "Let's head for the kitchen and see if someone there can lend us a dish to collect the snow in."

The chef was very sympathetic with their problem. "You had better let me take care of getting the snow," he told them. "But while I'm doing that, see if you can rustle up something to make a fire with. We'll need paper and wood."

Paul and Kathy left the diner and walked slowly toward the coaches.

"I've got a magazine we can use and a balsa wood model. That's a start," Paul said.

"Yes, but where will we find more wood?"

Paul had never before been so aware of the amount of metal on a streamliner. Doors, walls, tables—all metal. In the coach next to the coffee shop Paul's eyes settled greedily on an old man's cane. He turned away, feeling a little guilty.

Suddenly, Kathy stopped short and leaned close to him. "You see that lady sitting in the middle of the car on the left?"

"What about her?"

"She's knitting."

"So?"

"Her needles are *wooden!*"

"What are we going to do? Run up to her and grab them?"

"We'll explain why we need them and ask if she'll give them to us," Kathy said.

72

"You ask her. I don't think I can."

"Paul, Betsy's *got* to have some milk!"

"Okay, okay. I'll go with you. But you do the talking."

As they started up the aisle in the direction of the knitting woman, Paul had an inspiration. "Wait a minute. The lady I sit next to knits all the time."

"What kind of needles does she use?"

"I can't remember. But we can find out, and asking her wouldn't be so hard."

Kathy was glad to go along with Paul's idea. Luckily, they found Mrs. Green Dress in her seat, knitting. But their hopes collapsed when they saw that she was using metal needles.

Paul poured out the story of their problem just the same. Mrs. Green Dress put down her knitting and rummaged through her purse. A careful search produced only a package of cardboard nail files. "These aren't much," she said apologetically. "But you're welcome to them." Her hand sprang suddenly to her neck. "Ha! These are wooden." She unfastened a necklace of bright blue-and green-painted beads and placed them in Kathy's hand. "I don't know how well they will burn, but take them, dear."

Paul collected his magazine and model and handed them to Kathy. He decided not to contribute his drawing pad, at least not yet. Mrs. Green Dress left her seat and walked up and down the aisle asking people for contributions. She brought back a newspaper, two magazines, a child's six-inch ruler, several pencils, a coat hanger, and two clothespins. Kathy accepted them gratefully.

"You need much more wood, children," Mrs. Green Dress said. "And I have an idea where you can find it. There may be a few wooden hangers in each bedroom closet. Ask in each room if you may have them. I'll come with you if you feel shy about asking people for them."

"I don't mind asking. It's my sister who needs the milk," Kathy said.

"How about using the paddle that goes to your paddle-ball? Remember, you were playing with it yesterday?" Paul reminded her.

"Hey, good idea."

"You go on ahead, get the hangers and the paddle and I'll drop off the rest of the things with the chef," Paul suggested.

Kathy agreed, dumping all their treasures in Paul's hands, and disappeared through the rear door of the coach.

Paul was amazed at how quickly she returned to the kitchen with her paddle and a half dozen coat hangers.

The chef was impressed with their efforts. "You did well. Now let's hope this stuff gives us enough heat to boil the water. We don't want your baby sister getting sick."

He tore up the magazines and newspapers, twisted the pieces into tight rolls, arranged the paper and wood in the coal-burning stove. Then he lighted it with a match.

On top of the stove was a large pot filled to the top with tightly packed snow. Kathy, Paul, and the chef stood quietly watching the pot. For a long while nothing seemed to be happening. Paul enjoyed the warmth of the fire, but he began to wonder if the snow would ever melt. Then he noticed that the snow was moving away from the sides of the pot and sinking lower. Lower and lower it sank until its surface cracked and split into three islands that floated on the water underneath.

The fire was getting low. "Get a trainman to bring me a sledgehammer," the chef ordered.

Paul had no trouble finding a trainman, who opened a case of emergency tools to get at the hammer.

"Stand out of the way," the chef told them when he had the hammer. He broke up his large bread board with a few powerful strokes. "Now we've got wood enough to boil this water."

He was right. Before long the water in the pan began to bubble. The chef poured some of it in the bottle to wash it, and some over the nipple. Carefully he mixed water and milk together and boiled the mixture for a few minutes, then he poured some into the bottle.

"Tell your mother I've got enough milk for several more bottles," he told Kathy. "And don't run back too fast. That bottle needs a chance to cool down."

Betsy was crying so frantically when Paul and Kathy returned to the bedroom that she didn't even stop when Mrs. Cummings put the bottle in her mouth. But as soon as the warm milk began to trickle down her throat, she sucked eagerly and curled up contentedly in her mother's arms. Paul liked seeing the desperate look leave Mrs. Cummings' eyes and the muscles in her face relax.

"Oh, Paul, I'll never be able to thank you enough," she said, smiling.

Paul smiled back, feeling happy and proud of himself.

10

The Dark Moves In

BUT PAUL'S HAPPINESS was quickly shattered. He and Kathy had decided to play cards in the club car. They opened the door to find the fat man confronting the conductor.

"I thought you told us food was coming." The fat man's voice was harsh.

"We were all hoping some supplies would reach us before night," the conductor explained patiently.

"Can't someone send a helicopter to drop something to us?"

"Nothing can take off in this storm."

The fat man threw his hands in the air. "Oh, that's just great. You've got two hundred passengers sealed up in this frozen tin can with no lights, no water, and no food!"

"I've brought you an emergency lantern, and we should be getting a little warmth in here soon from the emergency heating generators under the cars. As a matter of fact, that's what I was checking on when I started through here. So if you'll excuse me . . ."

The fat man had nothing more to say. He dropped

into a chair and pressed his stubby hands against his forehead. Gloom descended on the car. The white-haired lady and the woman with the purple coat huddled together under a blanket, their figures casting heavy black shadows against the rising wall of snow at the window.

Paul and Kathy started a game of rummy, but they had trouble playing with their mittens on, and the car was so cold that they couldn't bear to keep their mittens off for long.

In spite of the heavy socks he had put on, Paul's feet and ankles pained him. He tried sitting on his feet. That helped, but after a while they felt so cramped that he had to stand up and stamp on them. He tried sitting on one foot at a time. That didn't work very well either. The foot that was on the floor got so cold that he tucked it under him before the other foot warmed up. Maybe he had better move his feet instead. He raised and lowered his heels. Up, down. Up, down. Then he tried swinging his legs under the table. But nothing helped for more than a few minutes.

Somehow, I've got to hang on, Paul thought. He shivered. The night seemed to stretch endlessly ahead. Would he ever leave this train?

He scrunched his fingers together inside his mittens, trying to get them warm. He stamped his feet up and down, untied the socks around his ankles, rubbed his ankles vigorously, then retied the socks. But he couldn't make the damp, penetrating cold go away. He couldn't make the emptiness in his stomach go away, either.

78

"At least your baby sister isn't hungry anymore," Paul told Kathy, trying to take his mind off his own stomach.

"I wish I could stop thinking about food," Kathy said.

"I wish I had a huge dish of spaghetti and a big cup of cocoa," Paul said longingly.

"Before long we may be eating mice and shoes and each other—just like the first Donner party." The fat man's shadow loomed over the seated passengers as he paced up and down the aisle.

"Don't say such things!" the white-haired lady said.

"It's the truth! George Donner and the settlers he was leading were trapped in the Sierra by a snowstorm, just the way we are, and not far from here, either."

"That was 1846 and they were on foot," said the woman in the purple coat.

The fat man paused beside her seat. "They were in a wagon train and I'd guess it was better in snow than this train."

Paul could hardly bear to listen to the conversation. He would have left the car but he was afraid that the coaches had no emergency light in them and he didn't want to start sitting out the long, cold night in the dark—at least not yet.

The fat man resumed his pacing. Paul knew he had to move, too. But where? He didn't want to chase the fat man up and down the aisle.

Then Kathy said, "Let's play Simon Says. Maybe it'll warm us up. You can be the leader first."

Paul stood opposite her in the aisle, bending, stooping, jumping, concentrating hard on the game to get his mind off the starving, snowbound settlers that the fat man had told about.

The door opened and in strode Mr. Walton, a heavy coating of snow still clinging to his parka. His face was as red as raw meat and wet from the melting snow dripping off his hood. His eyes and nose were running from the cold. The other passengers crowded close to him. The lady with white hair peered at him as if she couldn't believe he was real. Everyone started talking at once.

"You made it! You actually made it," the fat man exclaimed above the hubbub.

Mr. Walton pushed his hood back. One side of his face was lighted by the emergency lantern while the other was shadowed. His eyes looked sunken. The passengers quieted as he began to speak. "I can't tell you how terrible this storm is. I've tracked through snow all my life, but I've never seen anything like this. I sank down a foot with every push of my skis." He stared ahead as if he were still battling the storm.

"Did you get to a phone?" the fat man wanted to know.

"Yes, I did."

"What did you find out?"

"We're not abandoned."

"Did you send the telegrams?" the fat man asked.

"Yes, and I talked with the railroad superintendent. A lot of people are working night and day to get us out of here."

"That's comforting," the white-haired lady said.

"Yeah, but what are they *doing?* Specifically?" the fat man almost shouted.

"If the weather lets up, a Coast Guard helicopter will take off from Colfax to rescue some of us or bring in supplies. Highway crews are out in full force, but the snow closes in as soon as they plow it."

"What about those famous relief trains the conductor likes to tell us about?"

"Two of them are headed our way. One coming from the east, one from the west. They've both got rotary plows in front of them to clear the way. A freight is coming from the west, too, loaded with weasels, which could carry us out of here and onto a relief train."

"Weasels?" Paul could hardly believe his ears. "But they're just little tiny animals. They couldn't carry us . . ."

Mr. Walton leaned back in his chair and laughed. Then he moved forward, resting his hands on his knees. "Not that kind of weasel, Paul. The kind I'm talking about is something like a tractor with very wide treads over the wheels so it can easily ride over the snow."

"When do they figure on getting here? Three, four days? . . . a week?" The fat man couldn't control his sarcasm.

Mr. Walton turned to face him. "Look. I know how you feel. Don't think for thirty seconds that I like being cooped up here any better than you do. But you don't know what fighting this storm is like. Walk up to the baggage car and go outside for five minutes.

Try to walk against that wind."

Paul couldn't get rid of the feeling that the train was at the end of the world, and no one could ever reach it.

The fat man slumped into a chair.

"Look here. I've got to change into drier clothes and we'd all better get some sleep," Mr. Walton announced matter-of-factly as he rose and left the car.

Soon most of the other people in the club car headed toward their beds.

"I'll see you tomorrow, Paul," Kathy called as she left.

Paul realized that only he and the fat man had seats in the coaches, and the fat man showed no signs of moving. So Paul set off to find his seat alone.

The emergency lantern gave him enough light to get to the door of the club car. But once in the frigid vestibule, he was in total darkness.

Walking to the next car was simple when he could see where he was going. But in the dark, with the train tilting in toward the mountainside, it was a frightening journey. Paul inched ahead, keeping his arms stretched ahead of him. His left hand brushed the side of the narrow opening where the cars connected. The door into the next car must be straight ahead. Reaching forward, his hands touched glass. Glass that must belong to the window in the door. But where was the bar to open it? Underneath the window. Here! Gratefully he pushed the bar and the door opened into the dark, deserted diner.

Paul leaned against the inside of the cold metal door and took a deep breath. Could he make it all the way to the other end of the car? He knew that all he had to do was walk straight ahead. But to walk blind . . .

He wanted to scream for help. Instead, he forced himself to walk slowly forward, one step at a time, reaching out for the edges of the tables to keep himself on course. The car seemed endlessly long. Another vestibule. Then the long passageway beside the kitchen and down the aisle of the coffee shop.

When he reached the first coach, he was grateful to feel the presence of other people. Often, though, as he groped for the backs of the seats, he touched a head or an arm instead, and the person he had touched jumped at the sudden contact.

Paul began to worry about finding his own seat in the next coach. It was about halfway down the car on the right. But how would he know when he came to it?

Luckily, two porters were walking through his coach. One carried an armload of blankets. The other carried an emergency lantern, which filled the car with huge, eerie shadows. But it helped Paul to his seat.

"We'll be warmer if we share our blankets," Mrs. Green Dress said as she spread the three blankets over them. Paul edged close to her, so cold that he forgot to feel strange about snuggling up to someone he didn't know very well.

His thoughts kept going back to his mother, to the way she used to sit on his bed every night before he went to sleep and ask him how his day had been.

Tears began to sting his eyes, and a lump that he

couldn't swallow down filled his throat. Mrs. Green Dress seemed to sense how he felt, for she reached over and patted his knee.

That did it.

His tears fell in a torrent. He no longer had the strength to be brave. If crying was babyish, he just couldn't help it. He wanted to go home, and he ached with loneliness and cold and fear.

Mrs. Green Dress held him tightly. "There, there. It'll be all right."

The comfort of her arms around him made him cry even more. But after a long while his sobbing wore itself out and he just wanted to blow his nose. He pulled away to get out his handkerchief.

"I know how you feel. I'd like to have a good cry myself. Lyda may be having her baby right now, and I want to be near her," Mrs. Green Dress said. She didn't jabber on and on as she usually did. She tucked the blankets around Paul and moved close to him so he could rest his head against her shoulder.

The car was almost pitch black and strangely quiet, for the snow packed around the Flyer muffled the violence of the storm. But every few minutes weird, creaking noises broke the stillness.

In this icy nightmare even time seemed frozen. Paul's only comfort was the warmth of Mrs. Green Dress beside him. He pressed close to her and shut his eyes, hardly daring to hope that sometime he could have a hot meal and sleep in a warm bed again. The sounds of heavy breathing and snoring meant that most of the passengers were asleep.

Then Paul began to smell gas.

11

"Conductor, Hurry!
Something's Wrong!"

PAUL WASN'T SURE the smell *was* gas at first. The coach had almost no ventilation. Snow was piled to the middle of the windows and they were sealed anyway, so that opening them was out of the question. The car had a strong people smell. But now it had a new odor.

Paul sniffed. He sat up straight and looked around. No one seemed to be stirring. He sniffed again. It was a gas smell. His mother had had a gas leak in her stove once. This smell was like that.

Mrs. Green Dress was snoring softly. Should he wake her? Suppose it wasn't gas at all. Maybe he was imagining it. He sniffed again. It must be gas.

He flung off the blankets and stumbled over Mrs. Green Dress. He groped his way to the coach behind, pushed open the door, whanged his knee on the edge of a seat, lost his balance, and fell into a man's lap.

"Huh? Hey! What's going on?" the man cried.

"I'm sorry." Paul got quickly to his feet.

"What are you doing, crawling around in the dark?"

"I've got to find the conductor, or a porter," Paul said urgently, rubbing his throbbing knee.

"Something wrong?"

"I'm not sure. I think I smell gas."

The man sniffed. "I don't smell anything."

"Not here. In my car. The one ahead."

The glow of an emergency lantern showed through the glass of the door at the opposite end of the car.

"I think someone is coming who can help," Paul said.

"Do you want me to go with you?" the man asked.

"I'm okay." Paul was already making his way up the aisle toward the light.

When he reached the door, he found a porter talking to the conductor. Paul burst into the midst of their conversation. "I think I smell gas! In the front coach."

"Gas? Could something have gone wrong with the emergency heaters?" The conductor started to move as he talked. He led the way through the coach, his light held low so Paul and the porter, following behind, could see where they were going.

No sooner had he opened the door to Paul's car, than the conductor snapped out orders. "Go toward the rear," he told the porter. "See if any other cars are affected. Wake everybody up and get them out into the vestibules if you smell any gas."

"Wake up!" he shouted. "We've got a gas leak in this car. Go to the car behind." The conductor walked briskly down the aisle, shaking everyone who wasn't already moving. "Wake up! Move to the car in the rear."

Right away, the quiet car became noisy confusion. Paul was trying to get to his seat. He wanted to make sure Mrs. Green Dress brought along their blankets and pillows. Suddenly, he was caught in the press of people moving toward him. He couldn't make any headway against the stream of traffic.

A voice came from the rear of the car, shouting over the hubbub. "Conductor! Hurry! Something's wrong in the bedroom cars!"

If something was wrong in the bedroom cars, did that mean gas had leaked in there, too?

Paul's head began to swim. His knees went weak. Strong arms grabbed him and half dragged, half carried him into the next car.

When morning finally came, it was lighter than the night had been, but not much. Snow covered three quarters of the windows now, shutting out most of the daylight.

The passengers of the two coach cars were now jammed into one car with three, sometimes four, people squeezed into the space meant for two. Paul was squashed in with a strange man and woman. He was glad he was on the aisle, because this gave him a little more room. But it also meant that only one side of him was even slightly warm.

His body ached with exhaustion and cold. Wearily he tried to sort out what had happened the night before. He remembered hearing someone say, "Something's wrong in the bedroom cars." Pushing aside the blanket that covered him, he stood up. His head felt light. But he had to find Kathy, he had to make sure that she and her family were all right.

He made his way slowly toward the rear of the train. When he came to the bedroom cars, his heart sank. Something was wrong all right. The doors of the bedrooms had been smashed open. Some were hanging from one hinge, others were off completely. No one was left in the car. Were all the bedrooms like this, Paul wondered?

Fearfully, he entered the next car and found, to his horror, the same dreadful scene. Was Kathy's car like this? Had people come crashing into her room during the night to drag her and her mother and Betsy out? Paul could hardly bear to open the door to the next car.

But this car looked perfectly normal, its doors were tightly shut and intact. The next car looked normal, too. Paul walked up to Kathy's door and was about to knock when he thought better of the idea. Suppose she was still sleeping, why wake her?

Feeling a little faint, Paul decided to go into the observation car and sit down. The car looked like a refugee camp. Most of the passengers were huddled under blankets. Many of them had ripped up their bedsheets and wound them around their feet and legs. One man had taken curtains down from the windows and tied them over his shoes. No one talked much. Paul sank down on the floor near the door.

He was looking grimly into space, his mind a blank, when he heard a cheery voice. "Good morning, fellow Eskimos. How are things in the igloo today?"

Paul looked up to see Mr. Walton striding into the car. Paul grinned. "Hey, Mr. Walton, there's room over here," he said, patting the floor beside him.

"What say we harness our reindeer to this old train, Paul? Maybe they could pull it out of the snowbank." Mr. Walton sat down beside Paul and reached for his pipe. He put it in his mouth, but didn't light it.

"I think we need a herd of elephants," Paul told him. "Elephants on skis!"

"Perhaps you don't realize that we were nearly gassed last night," a woman snapped. She was hunched under a gray blanket.

"I do indeed realize it," Mr. Walton answered. "We have many dangers facing us. But we don't have to die of boredom."

"When we get to San Francisco, I'm going to sue this railroad," the woman went on.

"I think the railroad is doing all it can to help us," Mr. Walton told her.

"Help us! Is *that* what they're trying to do? Gassing people is a strange way to help them."

"No one was trying to gas us. The emergency heaters under the cars were turned on to keep us from freezing. Unfortunately, the snow clogged up the exhausts and gas leaked back into some of the cars."

"How are the people who had to be taken out of their compartments?" Paul asked.

"Some of them are still pretty sick," a dark-haired young airman answered. "That doctor on board rounded some of us up to save those who had locked themselves in their compartments. Some of the people were pretty far gone when we got their doors

90

broken down. We had handkerchiefs tied across our faces and we dragged the people out to where they could be given artificial respiration."

"Anyone here want breakfast?" A porter stood at the door.

"Breakfast? Really?" Paul couldn't believe his ears. He hadn't eaten anything since the skimpy lunch the day before.

"That's what I said. Some skiers got through to us and brought food in their knapsacks. It's in the dining car. Come and get it."

No one lost any time getting to the dining car. No roses decorated the tables now. The tablecloths were stained. The waiters' white coats were soiled and rumpled and partially covered by heavy jackets. No one cared. Food was more important.

"And it's hot!" the waiter exclaimed, as he placed a steaming bowl of oatmeal in front of Paul.

"How did you manage that?" Paul asked.

"Those track workers lugged sacks of coal for the stove on their backs from Crystal Lake," the waiter explained.

Paul felt that he had never eaten anything more delicious than that oatmeal. His bowl was soon empty. "May I please have some more?" he asked.

The waiter shook his head. "Sorry, son, no seconds. I hope we'll have something for your lunch, though. Take your dishes and silverware with you and bring them back at lunchtime. We haven't any water to wash them, you know."

Paul took his dishes to his coach seat, then stopped in the club car. He looked over the crowd. Kathy was nowhere around, but he recognized the fat man, the lady in the purple coat, and Mr. Walton, who was busy organizing an amateur show.

"Doesn't anyone in this assembled congregation have a guitar?" he asked in a voice that carried all over the car. "Flute? . . . Drums? . . . Piano? . . . Paul, surely you have a grand piano tucked away in your back pocket."

Paul smiled and shook his head.

"How about a harmonica?"

Paul shook his head again. "I don't even play an instrument."

"Foiled again," Mr. Walton said in mock sadness.

Paul was still worried about Kathy. He knew he would feel better if he could see with his own eyes that she was all right. He hated walking back through the train, but he forced himself to do it. With almost no ventilation and with toilets that wouldn't flush because the plumbing was frozen, all the cars had a foul odor. Paul walked as quickly as he could, hoping the smells wouldn't make him sick to his stomach.

Kathy opened the bedroom door when he knocked. "Hi," she said casually.

Mrs. Cummings was sitting on the bed, wrapped in blankets. Betsy was asleep beside her.

"Er—I wondered if you were all right. Was there gas leaking into this car?"

"The gas didn't get into our car," Kathy said. "But all night long I kept hearing yelling and moaning and people running back and forth in the corridor. It was awful."

"Mr. Walton is organizing an amateur show in the

club car," Paul said. "Can you think of anything we could do in it?"

"Why don't you two go into the observation car and see what you can come up with," Mrs. Cummings said. "I'm going to see if I can sleep a little."

12

The Amateur Show

AS THEY WALKED toward the rear of the train, an idea began to sprout in Paul's mind and he wondered what Kathy would think of it. "Would people on the train like to watch me draw?" he asked.

Kathy shook her head. "You ought to make it more interesting than just drawing a picture and having people watch you."

Abruptly Paul stopped walking. He turned to face Kathy. "I've got a good idea," he announced. "But first I've got to talk it over with Mr. Walton. Now, let's think what *you* can do."

"Me?"

"Sure."

"I wasn't planning on doing anything."

"You can make up stories. You like to dress up."

Kathy looked thoughtful.

"I'll bet you can come up with something really good," Paul told her. "I'm going to hunt up Mr. Walton now. Want to come?"

Back in the club car, Paul and Kathy talked over their ideas with Mr. Walton. "Right after lunch we'll start our show," he told them. "We'll save your part till last. Like dessert." His blue eyes twinkled.

Paul spent the rest of the morning sketching with his crayons and drawing pad. His hands were so cold that he had to draw with his mittens on most of the time. Every few minutes he would get up and walk around, hoping to get a little warmer. It didn't help much.

Outside, the storm continued relentlessly. The snow almost covered the club car windows. Would the train be buried completely?

"When are we getting out of here?" the fat man demanded as the conductor passed through the car.

"Just as soon as we can," the conductor replied evenly. "Some Sno-Cats from the electric company have brought us some more food."

"Wonderful. I hope the snow bunnies get through, too."

The conductor's eyes flashed angrily, but he kept his voice controlled. "Sno-Cats, weasels, they're all the same kind of thing—vehicles with treads on their wheels so they can ride over snow. The electric company needs them to repair their lines in weather like this."

"I'm glad to hear about them," the fat man said. "Do I understand that lunch is being served?"

"In the diner."

Lunch consisted of thick soup and bread. No seconds again, but Paul hoped he would be able to have some supper. The dining car steward didn't mention supper, though.

Paul found it hard to concentrate on anything ex-

cept the cold. It seeped through the floor, through his heavy shoes and socks. It crept under his coat, sneaked under his wool cap and mittens. There was no getting away from it.

Just as Paul moved into the club car, Mr. Walton started his amateur show. "Ladies and Gentlemen!" he called in his deep, resonant voice. "May I have your attention." The car quieted. "We have prepared for your enjoyment this afternoon the world's finest entertainment."

Many passengers clapped and cheered and stamped their feet.

Mr. Walton went on. "For our first number, let me introduce Mr. David Brooks, who hails from Balti-

more, Maryland, and his barbershop quartet. Let's give them a big hand."

Everyone clapped again, and four men walked to the front of the car near the kitchen. Paul remembered a barbershop quartet he had heard at home. The men had all been dressed in identical red jackets, black pants, black bow ties, crisp, starched shirts, and gleaming black shoes.

The train singers looked like tramps. They had thick stubble on their faces because they hadn't been able to shave, and they wore their overcoats. One of the men had heavy hiking boots on and another had one foot wrapped in a green wool scarf and the other one wrapped in a brown plaid scarf.

But when the men began to sing, Paul forgot how dirty and disheveled they looked. Their voices carried him far away from the damp, cold train.

> "I'll take you home again, Kathleen,
>   Across the ocean wild and wide;
>   To where your heart has ever been,
>   Since first you were my bonny bride."

Paul longed so much to be at home singing with his dad that he was grateful when the song ended and Mr. Walton began a recitation of "The Shooting of Dan McGrew." Now Paul was transported to the Yukon where

> "A bunch of the boys were whooping it up in the
>   Malamute saloon;
>   The kid that handles the music-box was hitting
>   a jag-time tune;
>   Back of the bar, in a solo game, sat Dangerous Dan
>   McGrew."

When he had finished, Mr. Walton bowed to the audience with an exaggerated flourish.

A fat lady in a fur coat waddled up the aisle. "What does the fashion-minded woman wear on a stranded train?" she asked shrilly, looking around at her audience for answers.

"A bearskin rug?" came the reply.

The fat lady laughed. "I wish I had one. But let me show you our January collection of Golden Flyer specials."

Ladies trooped in, each wearing a blanket in a

different way. One had a blanket draped around her shoulders like a fur stole. Another had fastened it on one shoulder with a big safety pin, cavewoman style. A third lady had the blanket covering her head entirely. She banged into one of the tables as she walked slowly down the aisle. "Oooooops," she said softly under her blanket and began to giggle.

"Easy there, girl," a man said, taking her elbow and guiding her into the aisle again.

The ladies strutted up and down the aisle while the other passengers clapped. Some of the men whistled. The women passengers laughed and said, "Just what I've always wanted" . . . "How gorgeous!" . . . "Now doesn't *that* flatter your figure."

Then the fur-coated lady intoned, "And now the Golden Flyer collection of fabulous footwear." A group of men trooped up the aisle holding their feet high in exaggerated poses to display the sheets, socks, towels, scarves, and curtains that were wrapped around them.

In the middle of the parade, the dining car steward opened the door to the car and announced, "Anyone in here want a chocolate bar?"

The models moved aside as the steward made his way slowly down the aisle, handing out chocolate bars as he went.

"How'd you get hold of those?" A man wanted to know.

"These are compliments of those fellas on the Sno-Cat," the steward explained.

"Why, it's a regular Charity Day at the Poorhouse," quipped the fat man.

"When do you figure we'll be out of here?" someone else asked.

"Maybe before dark. The conductor says that the western relief train is only a few miles away now."

"Oh, my," said the white-haired lady, "wouldn't it be wonderful to be out of here before night?"

Paul accepted the candy bar gratefully, admiring it for a minute, as he relished the anticipation of eating it. He held it up to his nose and inhaled the rich, clean chocolate smell. Then, slowly, he unwrapped one end. Biting off a square, he let his teeth sink gradually into it. He held the bite in his mouth while the chocolate dissolved into a thin stream of sweetness that trickled down his throat. Then he bit off another square. Paul made that candy bar last a long time.

A man with horn-rimmed glasses did a few magic tricks. He put a pink scarf in his hat, made it disappear, then pulled it out of his sleeve.

"I wish you could make this snow disappear," someone remarked.

"Let's do the bunny hop!" the lady in the purple coat suggested. "Come on, everyone, clear the aisle!" Some sat on the side and clapped and sang while others lined up in the aisle, each one's hands on the waist in front, and hopped down the aisle.

When the bunny hoppers became too breathless to hop any longer, Mr. Walton raised his arms for attention.

"Ladies and Gentlemen! We have a very special

treat for you." He waited for the noise in the car to quiet, then he continued. "We have on this train a group of very talented people. Not only do we have singers, magicians, models, and dancers. But we have an artist in our midst as well. Ladies and gentlemen, let me introduce Paul Sullivan. Paul, come here so everyone can see you." Mr. Walton extended his arm in Paul's direction. Paul felt his face redden. He wished he could run away and hide, but he tossed his hair away from his eyes with a jerk of his head and walked forward to where Mr. Walton was standing.

"Not only does our young artist have unusual talent," Mr. Walton said, "but he has suggested a way in which we can show our appreciation to the track workers who've lugged coal on their backs through this blizzard so we could have hot food. I'm going to auction off a group of Paul's drawings now. The proceeds will be given to those stalwart track workers."

Mr. Walton moved over to a table where Paul had placed his drawings. "We have here a fine desert scene. Just looking at it makes me feel warmer. How much am I offered for this splendid picture?"

"One dollar," said a voice from the opposite end of the car.

"One fifty."

"Three fifty."

Mr. Walton held the drawing over his head, turning it from one side to another so that all in the car could get a good look at it. "Only three fifty for this picture guaranteed to make you feel ten degrees warmer? . . . Who'll make it five?"

The drawing sold for seven dollars. Paul couldn't help feeling proud to be selling his pictures. A tall red-headed woman bought his pictures of the elephants with cats' heads and the butterflies with elephants' heads. She paid ten dollars for the two of them.

"What are you going to do with them, Vera?" Paul heard another woman ask.

"Do with them? I'm going to frame them and put them in Sarah's room, that's what I'm going to do with them."

Paul ached to be able to tell his mother about selling his pictures. She used to tack his drawings over the kitchen sink. "If I can't have a window to look out of while I wash dishes, I can look at your pictures," she often said.

Mr. Walton collected fifty dollars from selling Paul's artwork.

"How much did you get?" the fat man asked quietly.

Mr. Walton told him. The fat man reached into his pocket and pulled out two twenty-dollar bills and a ten. "You better make it an even hundred," he said, moving away.

Next Mr. Walton announced that Miss Kathy Cummings was available at one end of the car to tell fortunes. Paul saw that Kathy had arranged a scarf around her head, gypsy style, and wore big golden hoop earrings. She had even rouged her cheeks and put on lipstick.

While Kathy told fortunes, some people started card games. Mr. Walton led others in exercises, then

102

a community sing, "If you're cold and you know it, clap your hands. If you're shivering and you know it, stamp your feet."

Finally, the show wore itself out. The day was fading into another night and with it hopes of rescue faded, too. Depression settled over the car like a fog.

"Where are those relief trains?" the lady in the purple coat asked.

"The one from the west is getting close now," the conductor answered.

"What happened to the one from the east?" Paul asked.

"That was stalled in the snowdrifts."

"I thought we were getting out of here before dark," the fat man said.

"We'll get out of here as soon as we possibly can," the conductor answered quickly. "Better not get your heart set on leaving at a particular time, though."

The fat man didn't bother to comment. Stuffing his hands into the pockets of his overcoat, he strode out of the car.

13

"I Can't Stand It!"

No DINNER was served that night. The dining car steward assured the passengers that the chef had enough food to make breakfast in the morning, but he couldn't stretch the supplies enough to make two meals.

Outside, the storm still raged. Inside, the train was strangely quiet. Snow had drifted to the top of the windows, insulating the car from the wind's fury and, fortunately, from the worst of the cold.

Kathy went back to her room. But Paul delayed, trying to hang on to the jollity and fellowship of the afternoon, trying to while away time so that the night would be shorter.

He kept reminding himself that he was not going to pay any attention to the empty feeling in his stomach. The more he tried not to think of it, though, the more he could think of nothing else. Visions of hamburgers, squash pie, roast chicken, corn on the cob, hot dogs smothered with relish crowded into his mind to torture him. They made his mouth water and his stomach feel even emptier.

Even worse than being hungry was not being able to get away from the cold, which seemed to grow damper and more penetrating as time wore on.

The crowd in the club car was thinning out. Paul had a sudden fear that everyone would leave and he would find himself alone. So he groped his way forward to his coach car. Maybe he could get comfortable enough to sleep a little.

He found that he was more adept at walking in the dark than he had been the night before. During the day, he had carefully counted the number of rows from his seat to the doors of his coach. Now that information came in handy. He counted nine rows up on the right hand side and knew he had come to his place.

The track workers had shoveled away enough snow so that the outside doors at either end of Paul's coach could be opened to air out the car. That had gotten rid of the gas fumes, but it had made the car frigidly cold.

"I've got another blanket for us," Mrs. Green Dress said proudly.

"How did you get it?"

"A porter gave it to me. I think one of those Sno-Cats brought us a load of them." Mrs. Green Dress carefully arranged the blankets over herself and Paul. "I hope we can get more sleep tonight," she added.

Paul moved close to her. He didn't worry anymore about her asking about his family. He wouldn't even try to divert her attention now. He would just tell her the truth. All his earlier worries seemed silly now.

Nothing mattered but getting through the night.

The darkness was terrible, for it meant that he could do nothing but wait. Nothing distracted his attention from cold and hunger and the awful fear that help might never come.

Sleep was next to impossible. The slant of the train made him feel that he might tumble over and slam against the opposite wall. In spite of the blankets, he couldn't get warm. He couldn't get comfortable, either. He stretched out his legs so that his feet rested on the footrest in front of him, but that made his legs too cold. Yet when he curled them up under him, they became cramped and stiff.

Now that the outside doors had been shut again, the car smelled terrible. Even though the doors to the restrooms were kept closed, the stench from the toilets that didn't flush couldn't be contained. Paul buried his face in Mrs. Green Dress's coat sleeve. Her perfume, which had seemed so overpowering before, smelled good now.

He moved his watch from his left to his right wrist. He couldn't see the time, but holding the watch to his ear, hearing its steady tick, tick, tick, reassured him that seconds and minutes were passing. Yes, and if he could bear the waiting, hours would pass too, and the dawn would come.

Finally, he began to doze. He was home again, except that home was curiously different. Ice and snow were everywhere. He had to trudge through drifts to get from the living room into the kitchen. His mother was cooking dinner, even though a thick

106

coating of ice covered the stove. He tried to get a glass out of the cupboard, but the glass wouldn't move. It was frozen to the shelf . . .

"They can't keep us here any longer! They can't." The voice pierced the quiet. Paul was jolted awake.

"They can't keep us here!" The woman's voice was shrill with fear.

Mrs. Green Dress got up. Paul could hardly bear to have the warmth and comfort of her body taken away.

"I can't stand it any longer!"

Mrs. Green Dress spoke softly, soothingly, as she moved toward the voice. "It's all right. We'll get out soon. Don't worry."

"I can't stand it! I can't stand it!" the woman kept repeating.

Paul's thoughts hung suspended in midair. Tension gripped the whole car.

But Mrs. Green Dress was very calm. "I know. I know. Don't worry. We'll get out, you'll see."

Someone struck a match and in the brief glow Paul caught sight of Mrs. Green Dress putting her arms around the frightened woman. Then Mrs. Green Dress began to sing. Her voice wasn't pretty, it cracked at times. Often she forgot the words of the song and had to fill in the spaces by humming.

But as she sang, the woman quieted. Paul began to breathe normally again. The tension eased. Another voice joined in the song, then several more, until the words of the old Welsh air spread comfort like a soft blanket.

107

> "Sleep, my child, and peace attend thee
>   All thro' the night;
> Guardian angels God will send thee
>   All thro' the night,
> Soft the drowsy hours are creeping,
> Hill and vale in slumber steeping,
> I my loving vigil keeping
>   All thro' the night."

Paul drifted into a troubled sleep. He dreamed he saw policemen tramping up the aisle of his car. They were wearing orange raincoats, the kind they always wear in bad weather. "Come on," the policemen said. "We're coming to take you home."

Everyone on the train started to troop out. A steady stream of passengers filed past Paul, moving out of the train while the orange-coated policemen urged them to hurry.

Paul tried to follow, but he couldn't move. He tried to yell to them, but he couldn't talk. The stream of people moved on steadily. Paul tried and tried to get up, but he couldn't. The stream became a trickle, and Paul realized that the train was nearly empty.

"Stop! Wait!"

The passengers moved past him, wordlessly marching toward the exit.

"Wait! I'm coming. Don't go!" Paul screamed as loud as he could, but no sound came out of his throat. He couldn't raise himself up. All the passengers had gone. The policemen had gone away, too.

"Help! WAIT! Don't go without me!" He couldn't move, but he had to.

14

When Will the Rescuers Come?

ALMOST as if he were being raised in a slow elevator, Paul came up to consciousness. He felt cold and stiff. But he could move his head back and forth. He flexed his fingers. They moved too. He was still on the train, and Mrs. Green Dress was beside him. He wasn't alone.

Better still, daylight had finally come. Although the coach was still dark, the pitch blackness was gone. Even being able to see dimly was a help.

Paul got up and walked toward the coffee shop. He met the conductor at the door. Instead of the grim look of weary patience that he usually wore, the conductor was smiling. Did that mean that help had finally come?

"Are we going to be able to leave the train soon?" Paul asked.

"That's a real possibility now. The storm is over and the sun is out. You can go outside if you like and get some fresh air into your lungs."

Paul felt a Christmas morning excitement as he made his way through the baggage car to the outside door, the only door from which people could leave the train.

He walked into a brightness that was almost blinding. The wind had died, but the sharp, cold air made his face sting. Steep cliffs, draped in glistening, diamond-studded snow rose on one side of the partly buried train. On the other side, the white quilted bank sloped down to valleys where clusters of evergreen trees cast long blue shadows.

The Golden Flyer looked like a huge, frozen monster. A mass of wind-twisted icicles hung like a mane from the locomotive and the helper engines.

Paul gulped the clean air. It made his chest hurt, but the freshness of it was wonderful.

A pathway led away from the train. Paul followed it, the packed snow squeaking under his feet as he walked. "Where does this go?" he asked one of the track workers who was leaning wearily on his shovel.

"To Highway 40. Or it will when the highway gets plowed out. How do you like this snow, eh?"

"Swell." Paul watched the little white cloud his breath made. He felt he ought to say something more, but he didn't know what, so he picked up a handful of snow and tried to pack it into a snowball. No luck. It was too powdery.

Abruptly, the mountain quiet was broken by a throbbing, beating sound. Paul stood still and listened, his eyes searching for the source. It grew louder. Then he spotted it. A helicopter! He watched it approach until it was almost directly overhead. Would it pick up the passengers one by one?

No. It hovered over the slope near the train. Large

110

packages were lowered by ropes and released into the banks of soft snow. Then the helicopter rose again into the clear blue sky and slowly disappeared in the distance. The track workers rushed forward to retrieve the packages and carry them into the train.

Paul was hungry, but coming back into the dank, foul-smelling train for breakfast was almost more than he could bear. Somehow he managed to choke down a little food.

Then he went outside again. Many passengers joined him, walking up and down the path to Highway 40, milling around while the track workers cleared the snow away up to the steps of the first coach.

Kathy came outside and Paul hunched his shoulders and raised his arms menacingly in slow, awkward movements. "I'm the Snow Monster," he growled, advancing toward her.

Kathy didn't move an inch. "*I* am the Snow Phantom," she announced. "Faster then lightning." And she was off, speeding down the path with Paul in pursuit.

An hour passed. One question hung in Paul's mind, "When will the rescuers come?"

The track workers shoveled the snow along the side of the train. They scraped away the drifts on the steps of the cars. After they had shoveled all they could, they tramped down the snow so that the passengers could leave the train easily once rescue came. But no rescuers were in sight.

Paul had a hard time controlling his impatience. Where were all those people who were supposed to come and take everyone to a relief train? Paul couldn't bear the thought of spending another day and night imprisoned on the icy mountainside.

Then a shout went up from the track workers. "They've broken through! We can get out!"

The news spread like flame through paper. For one moment Paul and Kathy stared at each other, hardly daring to believe what they had heard. The track workers raced forward toward the highway, down the path they had so carefully prepared. Paul, Kathy, Mr. Walton, and a crowd of other passengers ran after them. Nearing the highway, they saw a moving cloud of snow and heard the roar of a big rotary road plow. The plow came nearer and nearer until it pushed away the last snow barrier between Highway 40 and the path to the Golden Flyer. The passengers yelled and waved. The driver of the plow waved back, but he didn't stop. He turned around and headed away from them.

Paul felt as if he had been dropped down an elevator shaft. "Why didn't the driver stop to pick some of us up?" he asked.

"Don't you see what he's doing, Paul?" Mr. Walton answered. "The cut he's made through the snow isn't big enough yet for a car to drive up to us, turn around, and drive out. The plow has to make the road wider. Come on, we've got to collect our things."

They went back to the Golden Flyer for the last time. It was alive with activity, as the passengers packed up their belongings. Time, which seemed to stop for three days, had started again.

15

Like Kathy's Golden Sapphire

DURING THE BLIZZARD, Paul had begun to think that all his worries would be over when rescue came. But he was wrong.

Now that rescue was certain, all his old problems came back to haunt him. He had pushed Aunt Edith and Uncle Harold to the back of his mind, but he wouldn't be able to ignore them much longer.

The conductor had asked everyone to remain in his seat until called. Convoys of cars, he said, would be coming to pick everyone up. Those who were still sick from the effects of the gas fumes would leave the train first. But where would the cars take them? To a relief train? Would the relief train go directly to Oakland? How would Aunt Edith and Uncle Harold know when to meet a train that was over three days late? Paul wished he knew what was going to happen.

"I hope I can get to Lyda's house before she has that baby. Poor girl, she must be worried to death wondering what's become of me on this train. I was able to be with her for two weeks before Ellen was born and it's a good thing I was there, too. Tom had to go off at the last minute on a business trip. Honestly, I don't know why companies have to do that to families. You'd think that . . ." Mrs. Green Dress was back to her pre-blizzard self.

Paul did not respond to anything she said. He felt that what happened to him was of no concern to her. She had been kind and comforting during the storm. But now she obviously felt that he didn't need her anymore. She prattled on about Lyda, and Lyda's husband, and Lyda's house, and Lyda's little girl, and Lyda's new baby until Paul wanted to scream. Being able to see the family you loved was nice, he thought bitterly.

If only he could talk to someone. Mr. Walton would be just the right person, but his seat was several cars away. Kathy was way off in the bedroom cars. She wouldn't be any help now. She'd be all excited about seeing her father again, and Paul knew he couldn't bear to hear her talk about that.

He didn't have anything to read and he didn't want to get out his drawing pad because he didn't know how long he would have to wait before he left the train. So he did nothing but sit and stew.

Finally the conductor announced that everyone should proceed toward the front of the car. Paul dragged his suitcase through the coach and out into the dazzling daylight. As he walked down the path, he kept switching his suitcase from one hand to the other. But he was sure one or both his arms would break off before he reached Highway 40.

Then he was herded into a waiting automobile

with six other coach passengers that he didn't know. The car was deliciously warm. It moved slowly between mountainous piles of snow and, a few miles later, pulled up in front of a ski lodge.

Inside, a fire crackled and blazed in a huge gray stone fireplace. How beautiful it was! Paul joined the group in front of it, admiring the way its orange and lavender flames licked the blackened logs. The chill and tension of the last three days began to melt.

Nearby, a table was spread with hot soup, coffee, and sandwiches. Paul ladled himself a cup of the tomato soup, picked up a couple of tuna fish sandwiches, then went back to his place by the fire. The lobby was becoming crowded as more carloads of passengers arrived. They were a rumpled, sorry-looking lot, bundled up in odd materials and bulging from extra layers of clothing. The men were unshaven, and everyone needed a bath and a good night's sleep. But they were beginning to relax and even to joke about their ordeal.

"How goes it, Paul?" The hearty voice belonged to Mr. Walton.

"I think I'm slowly defrosting."

"I know what you mean. It'll be a while before those poor chaps feel normal again." He gestured with his pipe toward a group of men slumped in armchairs, their faces sagging from exhaustion.

"We owe our lives to those men," Mr. Walton went on. "They're state highway department workers, and they've been battling this snow for five days, trying to keep the roads open. Monday they had to give up. They couldn't see their gloves in front of their faces.

116

Their rotary plow wandered off the road, went over a bank, and got stuck in the drifts. How they rescued it I'll never know. But they did. Dug it out with hand shovels yesterday. Then they worked all night to plow out twelve- to fifteen-foot drifts on Highway 40 so that we could get up to this lodge."

Paul watched the men sip their coffee. A group of passengers shook their hands and thanked them for their help. But the highway workers seemed too tired to do more than nod and smile.

A slim, blond bellboy approached Paul and Mr. Walton. "If you'd like to wash up a bit, I'll show you to a room," he said.

Using soap and water had never been one of Paul's favorite pastimes, but now it seemed like a wonderful idea. The bellboy carried Paul's suitcase into a pleasant room with a double bed.

"If you need anything, just call the office," the bellboy said, gesturing toward the phone on the dresser.

Left alone, Paul stood in the center of the room for a few minutes and just looked around. His long nightmare was finally over. The floor he stood on was flat. He had stood on flat floors all his life and taken them for granted. But now he knew what it meant to live on a slant twenty-four hours a day for three days.

He walked to the wall and flicked the switch. The light beside the bed went on. Last week that would have seemed like nothing at all. Today, it was marvelous.

In the bathroom, clean, sparkling water poured out of the sink faucets. Paul filled a glass and drank it slowly and gratefully. Then he filled the tub, undressed, and stepped in. He rubbed soap all over himself and lay full length to soak up the luxury of warm water on his bare skin. Maybe, he thought, his trip on the Golden Flyer was like Kathy's golden sapphire. It had made ordinary things seem special and precious.

He rubbed himself dry and dressed in clean clothes, thankful that he needed only *one* pair of socks, *one* sweater, and *one* pair of trousers.

By the time he returned to the lobby, all the passengers had been moved to the lodge. A trainman came up to Paul. "Would you care to send a message to someone. We're sending telegrams and making phone calls for passengers who want to let their families know they are all right."

Paul hadn't stopped to think before that his dad and Aunt Ethel and Uncle Harold must have been worried about him. "I guess they know we had some trouble."

"The radio and newspapers have been full of it."

Paul wrote out his father's name and address and Uncle Harold's name and address on the sheet of paper that the trainman handed him. Under his father's name he wrote, "I'm okay. Everything's all right now. I miss you. Love, Paul."

Under Uncle Harold's name he wrote, "I'm O.K. I think the train will get in to Oakland tomorrow morning. Love, Paul."

The trainman glanced at the paper as Paul handed it to him. "Yes, we will be getting in tomorrow morning. You can put on your coat now, because we'll be walking to the relief train in just a few minutes."

16

"A Message for You"

THE AIR OUTSIDE was icy, but exhilarating. The snow that had caused so much trouble for so many people looked deceptively innocent, wearing a beautiful, pink blush reflected from the setting sun.

The relief train, engines throbbing with power, was close by at Emigrant Gap. It was made up of pullman and dining cars only, which were warm, well lighted, and smelled good. By dusk the Golden Flyer's weary passengers were safely aboard, and the train rolled forward on the last leg of the journey to the West Coast.

Grateful as he was to be safe, Paul missed the friends he had made on the Flyer. He had spent five momentous days with them and now they had disappeared as if he had never known them. He caught sight of Mr. Walton at the far end of one of the pullman cars, but he was too far away to speak to. Paul didn't see Mrs. Green Dress or Kathy and her family at all. The bond that had united everyone while they were struggling to endure their common misery was broken now. Paul wished the break didn't hurt so much.

A banquet in the dining car, compliments of the railroad, took his mind off everything except eating. The tables were set with freshly laundered cloths and shiny silver. The goblets were filled with ice water. Paul couldn't decide whether he wanted fried chicken or steak, so the steward brought him some of each on a sizzling platter, complete with side dishes of green peas and creamy mashed potatoes with butter melting in a yellow pool on top. For dessert he had a huge square of chocolate cake with thick, chocolate frosting and pecans on the top. Every bite was delicious.

The three strangers sitting with Paul could talk of nothing but the storm.

"I don't think Reno is plowed out yet," said a middle-aged man.

"I heard the snow was 210 inches deep at Norden. Can you imagine, 210 inches deep?" The woman with long, blond hair, sitting opposite Paul, opened her blue eyes wide as she spoke.

"That's nothing," the woman's husband said. "One of those Sno-Cat drivers, you know, the guys who brought food and supplies to us on the Flyer, told me that near Donner Summit the 40- and 60-foot poles for the electric lines were buried!"

"I'm glad I don't live in Portola," the blond said.

"Where's Portola?" Paul asked.

"North of here, toward the head of the Feather River canyon. Their hospital is full of patients and they're running out of drugs. Short of food and fuel, too," the woman said.

"All those mountain communities are cut off by the blizzard, Almanor and Prattville," her husband added.

The middle-aged man wiped his mouth with his napkin. "I heard snow was so deep in that area that the roofs of some of the houses were buckling under the weight. Only way people could get out was to tunnel through their second-story windows."

The blond's husband began to laugh. "Did you hear about the woman who lost her backyard?"

Paul and the other two shook their heads.

"You know it's been raining outside of the snow belt. A lot of communities have floods."

"Was the woman's backyard flooded? What's so funny about that?" the other man wanted to know.

"Nothing's funny about it, really, except that it was so weird. This woman in South San Francisco was peacefully sleeping yesterday morning when the phone rings and it's her neighbor saying, 'Your property is coming into my yard.' So the woman jumps out of bed and sure enough her backyard is sliding downhill."

The blond arranged her knife and fork on her empty plate and rested her arms on the edge of the table. "You know, considering how terrible the storm was, I think we were pretty lucky on the Golden Flyer. I didn't think so at the time, but I do now. We've got a lot to be thankful for."

Later, when Paul slipped between the smooth

121

sheets on his pullman bed, he was thankful he didn't have to sleep in his clothes, thankful for being able to stretch out in a real bed. Worries about Aunt Edith and Uncle Harold still dogged his thoughts. But he was too tired and too comfortable to fret. He drifted into the most refreshing sleep he had had since leaving home.

The relief train arrived in Oakland well before dawn. The conductor had announced that no one needed to worry about leaving the train until morning.

Paul was awakened about seven thirty by a porter calling, "Paul Sullivan? Paul Sullivan?"

Paul stuck his head out of the heavy curtains around his bed, "I'm right here."

"Message for you. It was phoned into the station."

Paul opened the piece of paper that the porter handed him. "We'll meet you on the train platform at 8:30 this morning. Love, Aunt Edith," the note said.

At exactly 8:28 Paul left the train and stepped onto the platform, clutching his suitcase. He saw no one on the platform who could possibly be Aunt Edith or Uncle Harold. His heart beat rapidly and the palms of his hands began to sweat. Then he put down his suitcase and took a deep breath.

Five days ago, angry, frightened, and homesick, he had stood in another station, waiting for his journey to begin. Now it was finished. The trip had taken three times as long as it should have, and it had been three hundred times harder than he had imagined it could be.

Would living with Aunt Edith and Uncle Harold be worse than he expected too?

The trip on the Golden Flyer had been terrible, but not all terrible. Now that it was over and he could look back on it, he was almost glad he had had the experience. He wouldn't have wanted to miss knowing Mr. Walton, and Mrs. Green Dress, and Kathy, and her mother. His eyes were wet as he remembered how they had helped him when he needed it most. He remembered how much he owed to dozens of people whose names he would never know, the track workers, the drivers of the Sno-Cat, the highway men, the people at the lodge, the list went on and on.

But he had been able to help too. He knew how much Mrs. Cummings had appreciated the milk for Betsy, and he thought the track workers were pleased with the money from his pictures. Yes, and he had been the one to discover the gas leak in his coach.

Slowly, he pushed his hair out of his eyes and squared his shoulders. He wasn't pretending to be the conductor now. He was Paul Sullivan and glad of it. Living with Aunt Edith and Uncle Harold might not be easy, but he knew he could get through it.

A redcap rolled a baggage cart past him. The metal fastenings on one of the suitcases glinted in the sunlight. Paul looked hopefully up the long platform.

ABOUT SUSAN FLEMING

Susan Fleming is a free-lance writer who used to be a teacher and editor. Reading and the teaching of reading have been a special part of her life. She lives with her husband and two children in Massachusetts. This is her first book.